An excerpt fr

MW01268211

"Quit thinking the form," Sarah L. owner of the Michigan-based Lasting Impressions promotional firm, ordered from the desk to Taryn's left.

The form in question was the last step in registering for the annual Sugar Foot Island Songwriters Conference. Taryn had waited years for an invitation to the event. Considered it nothing short of a miracle that she'd finally gotten invited. Now, because of Brian's role as a conference sponsor, she had to turn it down.

"Don't make me come over there and fill that form out," Sarah warned. "I guarantee you won't like what I put in the 'other information' area. How does closet submissive in search of a dominant, whip-yielding bad boy sound?"

Taryn snorted. How it sounded was polar opposite of reality. She swiveled in her black leather chair to face her friend. "I just realized how much we have going on the third week of February. There's no way I can make the conference."

"Yeah, and I just realized how full of crap you are." Sarah rolled her eyes. Between their powder blue shade, her long blonde hair, and big boobs, she looked like the quintessential Barbie doll.

Apparently, Barbie never went out of style. Sarah had gone through no less than three guys this year, and it was still January. Not that going through men like they were chocolate on a high PMS day was a bad thing, but Taryn was still at a perfect zero for the year.

Or not so perfect, considering a mere glance at Brian's picture was enough to have her every hormone spiking with want.

LooseId®

ISBN 13: 978-1-61118-394-8
NOTHING ON BUT THE RADIO
Copyright © April 2012 by Jodi Lynn Copeland
Originally released in e-book format in May 2011

Cover Art by April Martinez
Cover Layout and Design by April Martinez

Printed in the U.S.A. by
Lightning Source, Inc.
1246 Heil Quaker Blvd
La Vergne TN 37086
www.lightningsource.com

NOTHING ON
BUT THE RADIO

Jody Lynn Copeland

Dedication

To my girls, young and old alike: you keep me going through the hard times and laughing through the best of them.

Chapter One

Five years had passed since she'd ordered Brian Macovney, aka Speedy Gonzales, out of her hotel suite following the most suck-tacular round of sex and confidence-jarring words ever. Five long years that felt like an instant the moment Brian's picture materialized on Taryn James's computer monitor.

Instant hurt and horniness went to battle inside her. Horniness won.

Taryn grumbled in acknowledgment of her tingling pussy. If she could look away, she'd be fine. But, damn it to hell, she couldn't pull her attention from his sexy-as-sin smile. With his thick, dark hair, vibrant green eyes, and five o'clock shadow that had a habit of showing up shortly after noon, he was everything she went for in a guy—lookswise. Personality-wise, he was an ass.

"Quit thinking about that prick and finish filling out the form," Sarah Langendor, Taryn's best friend and co-owner of the Michigan-based Lasting Impressions promotional firm, ordered from the desk to Taryn's left.

The form in question was the last step in registering for the annual Sugar Foot Island Songwriters Conference. Taryn had waited years for an invitation to the event. Considered it nothing short of a miracle that she'd finally gotten invited. Now, because of Brian's role as a conference sponsor, she had to turn it down.

"Don't make me come over there and fill that form out," Sarah warned. "I guarantee you won't like what I put in the 'other information' area. How does closet submissive in search of a dominant, whip-yielding bad boy sound?"

Taryn snorted. How it sounded was polar opposite of reality. She swiveled in her black leather chair to face her friend. "I just realized how much we have going on the third week of February. There's no way I can make the conference."

"Yeah, and I just realized how full of crap you are." Sarah rolled her eyes. Between their powder blue shade, her long blonde hair, and big boobs, she looked like the quintessential Barbie doll.

Apparently, Barbie never went out of style. Sarah had gone through no less than three guys this year, and it was still January. Not that going through men like they were chocolate on a high PMS day was a bad thing, but Taryn was still at a perfect zero for the year.

Or not so perfect, considering a mere glance at Brian's picture was enough to have her every hormone spiking with want.

He might not be dynamite in bed, but the man knew all the right moves to get a woman there. The way he kissed, with his whole mouth and that magical tongue... She shivered as sensual warmth zinged through her.

"C'mon, Tare. Don't even *think* about telling me you're going to let a guy who one"—Sarah raised the first finger of her left hand, flashing a French manicure and a heavily stoned ring—"never deserved you"—she raised a second adorned finger—"and two, sucks in the sack, destroy your dream."

"My making it in the songwriting industry doesn't depend on this conference. And Brian didn't suck, he was...abrupt." Right. And she'd just taken a fast trip to Fantasy Land.

"Maybe this isn't a do-or-let-your-dreams-die event, but it could be the chance to get your foot in the door. Not only do you have like a hundred songs that rock, but some of the biggest names in the recording industry are going to be there. You've said so yourself. Fifty times in the last two days, I might add."

Taryn's belly turned with the truth in her friend's words. No matter what she might pretend, Taryn wanted to attend the conference so badly she could taste it.

But was the cost worth the potential benefit?

The reason she disliked Brian wasn't because he was speedy in bed, or even that he hurt her emotionally, the way she'd led Sarah to believe. He hurt her in a much more lasting way. After getting off himself while leaving her hot and on the edge of orgasm, Brian told her she would never make it in the songwriting industry because she didn't come close to having what it took to write music. Then he backed that berating up with the biggest coup de grâce of them all. He claimed the words had come from his rock diva mother—Taryn's lifelong idol. Taryn had told herself he was full of shit. That he'd lied about his mother's words. Still that hadn't stopped the sting, then or now, as the hurt resurfaced to vanquish all trace of horniness.

"I want to go," Taryn admitted. "I just don't know if I'll be able to give my all when Brian's around." The ass would probably start laughing the minute he heard her lyrics. "Sugar Foot is not a big island. It's also only accessible by air or water. That means once my flight lands, I won't be able to leave without waiting for the next plane or boat out."

Sarah smiled knowingly. "You mean run, don't you?"

Hell no.

Taryn wanted to shout the words and knock the perceptive look off Sarah's face. She couldn't, because running was exactly what she'd meant. And that was just not right. She was no more insecure than she was a runner. But then, she also wasn't a woman who dwelled on one night of passion gone wrong. So why did that far from spectacular night with Brian continue to haunt her?

Was it just his claim of those cruel words coming from her idol, or was the attraction between her and Brian to blame?

While his stamina needed a megaboost, the sexual chemistry between them had been hot enough to set the snow falling outside the office windows on fire. The memory of his big fingers sinking inside her wet body came to her in a flash. A hot flash that left her panties damp and her pussy clenching.

Taryn puffed out a breath with the resurgence of desire. She was in serious need of a lay. "I can't do this. I'm not ready to put my songs out there." Unless... She turned an imploring smile on Sarah. Surely, she could handle facing any self-doubt Brian dredged up with the right moral support. "Will you go?"

"And push your songs? Ha-ha. Nice try, but I don't have enough talent to even attempt to get them to come across the way you mean them. No way could I win a contract for you."

"Not for me, with me. I'll buy your plane ticket. Pay for your room."

"I wish I could," Sarah said sympathetically. "But you're right about that week being busy. Not to mention the Wiccan Emporium has its grand opening the following Monday. Knowing how freaked out Laurel is about being accepted by this bass-ackwards, stuck-in-the-fifties community, we don't dare both take off."

As loud and attention grabbing as Laurel was, with her black Goth wardrobe and makeup and hair to match, Taryn had somehow managed to forget about her. The Wiccan could be the answer to her problems. Laurel had to know a spell to help Taryn breeze through the conference. Then again, if she knew spells that actually worked, why was she relying on a promotional firm to help her business take off?

Whatever the reason, it was the excuse Taryn had been looking for. "Told you that week's crazy. It's the absolute worst time I could be gone."

Sarah smiled in a way that said *I know what you're up to, girl, and it's not going to work.* "I never said it was crazy, just a little on the busy side. Even with juggling Laurel's freak-out sessions and the rest of the accounts, the workload's nothing I can't handle for a few days. If I need to, I'll get a temp.

"I can't go to Sugar Foot, but *you* can," Sarah asserted. "And you *are* going, Tare. There's no way, as your best friend and the person who has to save you from overdosing on Chocolate Cashew Heaven ice cream every year when you don't get an invitation to the conference, I'm going to let you miss it." She nodded at Taryn's computer monitor. "Finish filling out the registration form and hit the Submit button. You have thirty seconds, starting now."

"I'll have you know ice cream contains calcium, an essential part of the food pyramid." Besides, the layered look was a must for the winter months, and she always lost the weight she gained from OD'ing by swimsuit season. Well, all but the inches from her hips. Nothing could shrink the ax-handle size of those things. She knew; she'd tried every fix imaginable.

Taryn once more met with Brian's smile. Heat coiled in her belly. The kind of wickedly salacious heat that said the only safe thing to do was stay home. Pangs of disappointment shot through her as she closed the Internet browser window. "I can't go. I'm not."

Sarah gasped. "Taryn! I cannot believe you! You are one of the ballsiest people I know, and you're acting like a big chickenshit."

Big chickenshit, was it? Well, she always did believe in the phrase if the shoe fits... "What can I say, but...*bawk. Bawk, bawk, bawk...*"

* * *

Taryn sank back in Sugar Foot's version of a taxi, which looked more like an open-sided golf cart. Sarah's chickenshit analogy had brought her here. Taryn could accept she was running scared in private. Sarah's pointing it out aloud had been too much to tolerate. She was a woman who loved a challenge. If facing her past and getting over Brian's hurtful words once and for all wasn't a challenge, nothing was.

Hey, maybe she would get lucky and their reunion would last the same length of time as their first and last full-on sexual encounter—approximately one and a half minutes.

Smiling over the thought, Taryn took in the surroundings. The island was fifteen square miles with a plethora of white sand beaches. More than one of those beaches was clothing optional, and since she'd arrived two days early in the hopes of dealing with Brian preconference, she planned to pay at least one of them a visit.

Hopefully in the process of browning her buns, she would find a candidate for a week-long fling with which to break her recent dry spell. Or maybe she would find that candidate at one of the local clubs tonight. The sun already dipped low on the horizon, bathing the myriad tropical vegetation and the rolling sand cliffs in an orange-red glow.

The twin towers of the Seaside, the hotel that would house the conference, came into sight ahead, and Taryn leaned her head outside the taxi for a better view. The conference registration brochure called the hotel the ideal meeting place for business. The travel brochures she'd come across made it sound more like the ideal place for a torrid, steamy affair.

Along with queen-size beds and spacious bathrooms, rooms were equipped with a Jacuzzi and a waterside balcony. Tropical-themed balcony sex was a thrill Taryn had yet to experience...and too much not to fantasize over.

As the taxi continued onward, the sultry breeze toyed with her hair, pulling the silky black strands from her hairclip much the same way they would be lifted and carried on the breeze out on her balcony. She imagined herself seated there while some surfer boy toy devoured her with the heat of his eyes.

Darkness settled in. The wind picked up, grew cooler.

His gaze sizzled into her, coursing liquid longing through her veins to nestle decadently between her thighs. His attention drifted to her breasts, lingering as a visual caress, and her nipples stiffened to aching points. With featherlight touch, she stroked the straining tips through her black halter-style dress. A moan tugged from deep down to gasp from her lips. His eyes dilated, lips licking hungrily as she turned her fingers on the tie holding up the snug dress.

The knot gave way. The material fell, gathering at her ample hips and exposing the barest hint of pubic hair.

No panties? *His green eyes sparkled sexily with the unasked question.*

Responding only with a naughty smile, she returned her fingers to her breasts. Wind licked at the bare, sensitized flesh, heightening her pleasure, wreaking wondrous havoc on her nerves. A brush of her thumbs against the swollen pink points of her nipples careened erotic sensation to her core. This moan erupted loud and low, echoing into the night as her sex grew heavy with cream.

Voice thick with need, he demanded, "Take it all off. Let me see you."

Taryn's blood hummed, seemed to singe right through her veins. Hungry urgency crashed over her. She pushed from the railing and eased the dress from her hips. His gaze fastened on the slight hair covering her mound. The smugness of his luscious grin said he was pleased with her decision to forgo panties. Then he was right there, his big hands on her body, lifting her onto the railing. Her ass settled against the coolness of the wrought iron, a delicious contrast against her hot flesh. Then a hotter connection as he bent his head and sucked her nipple into his mouth.

He bit down on the crown, twisted to the point where pleasure bordered on pain. Shoving her fingers into his hair, she writhed on the railing. Silently pleaded to feel his lips lower, his short, dark stubble chafing her most intimate places.

That want didn't go unanswered.

Within seconds he released her nipple to trail his tongue down her belly, into the dip of her navel, around the damp hollow. A heated whimper left her as he separated the folds of her sex with his thumbs. A moment's hesitation to devour her slick opening with the intensity of his eyes and the hot whisper of his breath, and he sank his tongue inside her pussy.

Taryn's belly tightened as the slow fucking of his tongue turned to long, hard magnificent strokes.

Ah, God! So good. Exactly what she needed.

Gripping his hair, she tossed back her head and gave herself to his every desire, every succulent secret that waited in the darkness of night.

Juices of arousal leaked down her thighs, mixing with the briny tang of the ocean. Shamelessly, she parted her legs farther and panted out a demand for more. His eyes reflecting a wicked gleam, he worked his tongue faster, in and out of her dripping sex. Electrifying pressure built deep within her core. Her heart stampeded, slamming against her rib cage near painfully. Threatening to burst from her chest.

"We've reached the Seaside," a man said in a thick island accent devoid of sensuality.

Taryn's heart didn't burst, but her fantasy did.

She opened her eyes on a daze of confusion. The sight of the taxi's driver eyeing her as if she'd lost her mind quickly brought things back into focus. On the tail of that focus came disgust. She'd been fantasizing about the last man she planned to allow near her balcony, let alone her body.

Freaking Brian!

Mentally dousing her frustration, Taryn climbed from the taxi. A gray-haired hotel concierge, in casual white shorts and a light blue polo shirt with the hotel's white and navy crest on its pocket, loaded her suitcase and carry-on bag onto a wheeled cart. He followed her into the hotel and through a spacious sitting area decorated in cool blues and tans and populated with chatting hotel guests to the registration desk.

A young, tanned, smiling brunette came to the counter. "Welcome to the Seaside, Sugar Foot's premier vacation and meeting place. How may I help you?"

Noting the woman's name tag, Taryn returned her smile. "Hi, Ginny. I'm here for the songwriters' conference."

Ginny's smile lost its professional edge to turn conspiratorial. "Let me guess, you came early to take in the island's sights." Before Taryn could respond, she continued in an exuberant tone, "I don't blame you. I moved here a couple months ago, right after graduation. Mom about had a kitten over me moving so far away, but it was *sooo* worth it. This place has a ton to offer." She looked at the computer screen on her left. "To get you checked in, I'll just need your name and the credit card you reserved your room under."

"Great. My name's Taryn James." Taryn retrieved a credit card from her purse. "I'd like to check out the local nightlife. Any place in particular you'd suggest?" *Preferably somewhere the men are talented in bed and easy to get there.*

"Definitely. Check out the Strobe on the other side of the island. It's totally happening and, since I don't see a guy with you, where all the hotties hang out."

Perfect. A quick check-in, shower and clothes change, and she would be on her way to a long overdue lay. Her sex tingled with unbridled anticipation. She fought the urge to rub her hand over her crotch.

Mmm... Might have to add a pre-Strobe fingering to the mix. A little masturbation daycap.

"Taryn?"

The too-memorable male voice sneaked up from behind Taryn so fast, for a moment she thought she'd imagined it. Then Brian's unmistakable scent registered, and her smile vanished while her pussy ached for a much bigger, stronger finger.

Chapter Two

As if his sexy male scent wrapping around Taryn's better judgment wasn't enough, Brian's voice still sounded the same. Deep, husky. Too damned effective at dampening her panties and mushing her logic.

If she didn't turn around, was there a chance he would go away?

No acting the chickenshit, a little voice shouted from the back of her head. This meeting was destined to happen. It was good to get it over with quickly so she could enjoy the rest of her week.

Slowly, she turned from the safety of the reception desk and Ginny's warm smile. Standing face-to-face with Brian generated the same visceral response now as it had the first time she set eyes on him. Seductive heat pitched through her, and she found herself licking her lips.

At thirty-three, he was too young for much in the way of age marks. As far as Taryn could tell—and his red swim trunks, white tank top, and sandals afforded her a very nice viewing opportunity—he hadn't changed a bit.

Hell, her luck did not run to the good side.

Without a doubt, he still looked better than any Chocolate Cashew Heaven triple scoop cone. It was more than his chiseled good looks and the golden tan that made it clear he lived far south of her snowy, bitter Michigan winters. It was his stance, the self-assurance in his eyes. His very presence that seemed to command attention and not just of her mind.

Sexual awareness practically arced in the air between them. A second skim of his physical assets beaded her nipples against the lace of her bra. She sighed. If only his bedroom skills lived up to the promise of his appearance...

If only, nothing.

Even if he were the king of all that was hedonistic and carnal, he would still be a world-class jerk. If the nasty words he'd flung her way weren't testament enough to his callousness, then his career choice certainly was. What nice guy chose to be a corporate raider?

He was lucky she hadn't learned his profession before inviting him into her bed, or they would never have shared that brief interlude.

Taryn forced a smile. "Brian. I didn't expect to see you here."

"You didn't see my picture, along with the conference judges and other sponsors, on the registration form when you filled it out?"

There were other people on there? "I guess if I did, it slipped my mind."

He didn't look convinced, but dismissed it with a shrug. "So, how've you been?"

"Great. Business is great. I own a promotional company that's so busy I'm going to need to bring on more help soon. The past two years, I've sold over three dozen commercial jingles. Many of them have won national awards. My songwriting's..." His mouth kicked into a half smile, and she ground to a halt.

Nice. Not only was she rambling like an anxious little idiot, but spouting off her résumé in half-truth format. "What about you? Still getting your kicks by stealing companies out from unsuspecting noses?" She bit her lip. Damn it, too much time spent badmouthing Brian with Sarah was attempting to leave its mark.

His half smile became a full grin. "Hey, what can I say, I have a fetish for making other people's lives miserable."

"Nice to know you're good at something." Ugh. She needed to shut up.

He winced. "Our history's the reason I've been waiting for you to check in. I know it isn't the best, but I was hoping we could let bygones be bygones. You know, bury the proverbial hatchet, let go of old grudges, and all that?"

He'd been waiting for her? Did that mean he felt guilty over his behavior the last time they'd been together, in which case he was one step up from the cruel, quick-on-the-draw bastard who deserved every snarky comment she tossed his way?

Deserving or not, Taryn couldn't voice any more negative words. As a conference sponsor, he would be in direct contact with and have the power to influence the judges. "I'm not carrying any grudges, but whatever works for you."

She turned back to the registration desk to find Ginny waiting with a key card and her credit card. Taryn took them and, after Ginny told her someone would be up to her room shortly to see that everything was to her liking, she said her thanks to the young woman and turned back to Brian. They had their reunion moment. It was time to say good-bye and hope she never saw him again.

"I want to get settled into my room before it gets any later. Maybe I'll see you around." *Hopefully not.*

An unnamable emotion flickered through his eyes, softening them and freezing her on the spot. The typically dark shade of jade wreaked hell on her hormones. The currently soft shade of moss worked its way on her sympathy. She was nearly ready to apologize for her crack about his being good at something when his grin returned, edging toward cocky terrain.

He nodded. "You can count on it, Taryn."

* * *

Taryn James. Long black hair, deep blue eyes, slightly too-wide mouth, big breasts, and generous hips that combined to make a cock-rousing package. Brian's penis was still partially erect more than a half hour after their encounter at the reception desk. He still felt like beating the hell out of himself too.

What the fuck had he been thinking, suggesting he would make it a point to see her this week?

The plan had been simple: make clear his intent of letting the past go and then avoid her at all costs. While he wasn't directly involved in the music industry these days, he was one of the conference's biggest financial backers. The last four years he served as a judge for the end of the week performances as well. But the last four years Taryn's name hadn't been on the attendance roster.

His luck couldn't hold out forever.

Apparently, though, Taryn's grudge against him could. As could her memory of their one and only night together.

Their past had to be the reason Brian strayed from the plan and said he would see her around. He'd always wondered if he hurt her with his callous and completely untrue words. Today, he learned he'd hurt her enough for it to plague her for years. She came off as being too confident to care about what others thought. But, obviously, she wasn't. Obviously, she needed his apology.

Damn, he hated apologizing.

This time it wasn't just a sorry he would have to give, but an explanation as to why he acted the way he had.

Shitty job or not, Brian had to do it, and then he could get on with his week. As a restructurer and occasional buyer of companies on the verge of bankruptcy, the bulk of his time was spent conducting business. This once a year getaway to Sugar Foot afforded him a week of pleasure-filled nights. The kind of pleasure he wouldn't be experiencing with Taryn. He dealt with the dominant type too often through his business dealings. When it came to his pleasure dealings, he liked his partner on the docile and, therefore, far less demanding side of things.

Taryn didn't know the meaning of the word docile. She was an aggressor, and it was that trait Brian blamed on his lack of control the night they'd had sex.

They'd met backstage at one of his mother's concerts. Around his mother, Taryn had clearly been experiencing hero worship that masked her true self, because she'd come off as sweet and slightly insecure. Then he'd gotten her alone, and she turned into another person. With her brazen behavior and words, she had him climaxing before he'd even been able to get all her clothes off. He'd been embarrassed as hell and had lashed out at her in the most hurtful way he could think of to save his ego.

In short, he'd been an asshole of the highest order.

Making his way to the hotel room he'd overheard the check-in attendant tell Taryn was hers, Brian wished he'd let his ego suffer five years ago. Instead, it was about to take a pounding he'd have to relive all week long, whenever he had the misfortunate to pass by Taryn or hear that sexy-as-hell laugh of hers.

He didn't want to think about her laugh. He didn't want to think anything about her. And he wouldn't, just as soon as he got this one little dirty deed out of the way.

* * *

Despite her body's quaking desire for release, Taryn had forgone the daycap masturbation. Fear that she'd imagine Brian's face as she fingered herself to orgasm had her scurrying into the shower instead.

Now she applied a light application of makeup and finished with a mist of cinnamon-scented body spray.

The Strobe awaited her, complete with a bevy of island hotties, and a trio of extra-large margaritas. Or maybe she'd forget about the juice part of the drink and stick with straight tequila.

She'd been drinking tequila the night she met Brian, backstage at one of his mother's sold-out concerts.

Taryn halted midway to the closet where she'd hung her clothes, and frowned. Clearly straight tequila wasn't a good idea. Neither was thinking about Brian's mother. Jacqueline had died three years ago from an illness the paparazzi hadn't been able to get to the bottom of. Though Taryn had only met the rock diva once, five years before her death, she had seen the way Jacqueline treated Brian and everyone else who came into contact with her. The songstress hadn't been the type to knock another down. She never would have told Brian she thought Taryn incapable of making it as a songwriter.

Unfortunately, during that short visit backstage, Taryn had also seen the way Brian treated his mother. He'd really cared about her. The honest affection humanized him in a way Taryn didn't want to acknowledge.

She much preferred the evil version of Brian she'd built up in her mind. Brian the corporate raider who heartlessly stole faltering companies from their owners and sold them to the highest bidder, netting a generous profit. Brian who wined and dined women with magical words and an even more magical mouth just so he could get them in bed and then leave them on the edge of climax and aching for release. Brian who she wasn't going to waste her time thinking about so much as another nanosecond.

Due to the vital part he played in the conference, Taryn knew she would have to talk to him and agree to let the past go before the conference started up. And she would. Just not tonight.

Tonight was for her.

And her favorite red wrapper.

Smiling at the effect she knew the scarlet red number had on men, Taryn continued her trek to the closet and pulled it off its hanger. The outfit wasn't really a wrapper, but a dress so scanty, it could pass as one. Then there was the other reason she called it a wrapper, because whenever she wore it, the night ended with her naked and sweaty, and the dress wrapped around some lucky guy's bedpost.

After tonight, her celibacy streak would be long gone.

Tossing aside her robe, Taryn pulled the spaghetti strap dress over her head. Cool cotton slid over her naked breasts, rubbing her nipples into tight beads as the material settled into place. Lycra lined the bottom half of the dress, compressing her hips and ass into a package that didn't require its own zip code. The snug, short fit was enough to bring most men to their knees. When combined with spiked black stilettos that all but screamed "do me," the few strays fell into line.

A knock sounded on the door as Taryn was strapping the heels on. Remembering Ginny's words about someone checking in to see if Taryn found the room to her liking, she went to the peephole. A man stood with his back to her. While she couldn't see his face, the suntanned skin of the back of his neck and arms suggested he was a local.

Thrusting her shoulders back so her breasts pushed against the cotton and risked the limits of the dress's low-cut front, she pasted on an inviting smile and reached for the door.

There was no time like the present to try out the potency of her little red wrapper on an island hottie.

Chapter Three

No way in hell was that dress legal.

Too low cut, too tight, barely enough material in the skirt to cover her ass, not to mention how much of Taryn's generous breasts were thrust in Brian's face the moment she opened her hotel-room door. If the poor excuse for a dress was the kind of thing she planned to wear this week, he was in big trouble. The kind that had everything to do with walking around in a constant state of arousal.

His once-over ended on spiked heels that had the makings of "fuck me" written all over them. No woman he ever dated wore heels like that. Good thing too. If those women had been anything like Taryn, they'd have insisted on wearing the spikes to bed, and the night would have ended by either taking out one of his eyes or puncturing a family jewel. Even so, the idea didn't stop the anxious throb of his quickly swelling cock.

"Are you lost?" she inquired.

He brought his attention back to her face with the cool question. The siren's smile she'd worn upon opening her door was now a smirk.

It would be convenient to say he was indeed lost and get the hell away from Taryn and her tiny, electric red dress. But he couldn't. He'd come here to say something, and he would get the words out. "You look amazing."

Yeah, those weren't the words.

Her smirk softened, plumping full lips. "Thanks. I was about to go out."

"Right." Out. Obviously trolling and not for fish. Good. Let her impose her controlling nature on another man. She could bring the poor sap back here and proceed to dominate him all night long.

Brian's gut tightened. He didn't want Taryn, but he also didn't want to imagine her screwing some other guy. "Can I come in?" He looked past her into the room. "I won't take up much of your time."

She frowned, but then nodded. "Sure." After gesturing him inside, she closed the door, crossed to the bed, and sat on the end. "What's this about?"

The little red dress barely covered her thighs when she was standing. Sitting, the material came an inch, maybe two from revealing whatever she wore under it, if anything. His shaft hardened fully at the idea of her as pantyless. Her luscious pussy just a leg spread and a handful of feet away.

Cursing both his unruly cock and imagination, he jerked his gaze back to her face. "I never meant to hurt you, Taryn."

"I told you I don't hold a grudge. Besides, you didn't hurt me. We hardly knew each other when we slept together. Anything you said was forgotten the second you left my apartment."

Really? Then why was her posture suddenly so rigid it pained him to look at her? The urge to join her on the bed and rub the tension away hit him hard.

Too damned bad. She could tense up until her spine cracked, and Brian wouldn't sit on that bed with her. "No, it wasn't."

Taryn's eyebrows shot together. "*I* said it was. It's in the past, so leave it there."

"I won't leave it there, because I know it isn't in the past. You're lying to me, the same way I lied to you that night when I told you my mother said you didn't have what it takes to make it. She never said that. I never believed it." Scrubbing a hand through his hair, he blew out a breath. "Hell, I've never even heard your music. I know you gave Mom a CD with some of your songs on it, but whether or not she got around to listening to it that night or ever, I have no idea."

For an instant, her mouth gaped and hurt passed through her eyes. Then the look was gone, and she asked, "Then why did you say it?"

"I thought you didn't care."

"I don't, but now I'm curious."

Brian shrugged, doing his best to make light of the situation. "You weren't what I expected. Around Mom you came off as being sweet, even insecure. The minute we were alone and naked, that changed. You shocked me."

"You were expecting to find a man under my clothes?"

"Hardly." Not even the queen of drag could fake breasts as gorgeous as hers. "I'd just never been with anyone as aggressive as you. I wasn't prepared for you to be that way, or things would never have ended on such a fast note. I *always* satisfy my lovers, Taryn. What happened with you was a onetime deal."

She didn't look convinced. She also didn't look angry or even hurt. Her smile had softened into the sensual one she'd given him upon first opening the door.

What the hell was going through her head?

Beyond a couple hours of chitchat five years ago, he didn't know her. All right, he did know one other thing. When she looked at him that way, with carnal invitation shooting from her eyes and the curve of her shimmering red lips, keeping his brain from wandering to his dick was out of the question.

Taryn's lips curved higher, parting slightly to reveal a glimpse of damp pink tongue. Dangling her legs over the end of the bed, she reclined back on her elbows. "So, what you're saying is you're really great in bed, a paragon of sexual potency?"

Her tone was suddenly low, husky, inviting. As was the way the miniscule skirt of her dress shifted higher on her bare, white thighs with each little move.

Inviting and dangerous.

Brian dragged his attention up from her thighs to connect with the risqué plunge of her breasts. The way she sat had more supple flesh pushing over the neckline than staying in. The dark pink skin of an areola slipped into view. Her nipples beaded, pressing hard and erotically at the edge of the neckline.

Hot, large, spicy nipples that fit perfectly into his mouth.

He groaned. Hell, he couldn't even remember what they'd been talking about, and yet the memory of her scent, her taste, her feel beneath his tongue came to him like he just had her last night.

He recalled then; his skills as a lover. "I haven't gotten any complaints." Taryn raised an eyebrow, and he amended, "Aside from you."

She laughed. "I find that hard to believe. I think the odds are a whole lot better that you came here and told me this in the hopes of my giving your ego a second chance. I might find you attractive, and I might even be aware the chemistry between us could scorch water, but I'm not planning to sleep with you again, so you can forget about my helping to patch your fragile ego."

Brian's heart beat harder. The blood pitched through his body, hot and heavy, headed straight to aching balls. The laugh, damn it. She had to go and break out that laugh.

He bridled his fast-fading restraint. "I didn't come here for sex. I wouldn't want it if you offered." The raging state of his cock proved the words a lie, but a man had to say what a man had to say. "I came to apologize, and I did, so good-bye."

A smart man also knew when to run.

He swiveled on the heels of his loafers, forcing his steps to remain unhurried as he moved toward the door. She didn't scare him. The effect she had on both his libido and his common sense was more a thing of annoyance.

"Then again, it has been a long time since I've gotten laid." Taryn's words reached him as a seductive whisper when he was less than three feet from the door. "Too long. I was going to pick some lucky guy up at the bar tonight, but since you're already here, maybe I could revise my plans a bit and give us another chance."

Yeah, it was annoyance she made him feel, Brian thought again. Annoying as hell the way she stripped his better judgment and had him eager to turn around.

Have some willpower, man. Don't do it. Don't turn back.

To hell with the voice of reason. He was neither a saint nor a eunuch. Not turning back was impossible.

He spun around to find the sensual quality of Taryn's voice reflected in her eyes as lust. The blue was darker than ever. Her fingers stroked the mattress near her hip in a slow, sensual rhythm. Too easily he could envision those same fingers stroking her clit. "C'mere, big boy. Show me what you're capable of."

His dick twitched. Tightly, he asked, "You're joking, right?"

She drew her knees up on the bed, jabbing the killer heels into the mattress, and peered at him through the V of her thighs. "Do I look like I'm joking?"

Fuck. He couldn't tell. He also couldn't take his eyes off the black lace sheathed between her thighs and the sight of her bared butt cheeks. He couldn't see a lot from this angle, but plenty enough to tell she wore panties...of the barely there variety.

This was the reason he never messed with women like her. Not only did they always have to be in the lead, but they didn't play fair.

"I know you want to fuck me, Brian. I want that too." Taryn came to her feet in one fluid move. She reached for her itty-bitty dress straps. "I'll even get us started." She slid first one, then another thin red strap down her shoulders. She reached around behind her then. The subtle hiss of a zipper filled the room, sounding louder than a thunder boom.

"What are you...?" He couldn't get any more out before she had the dress unzipped and was lowering the top half to her waist.

She wasn't a skinny woman, but one whose body was a healthy balance of meat and muscle. He'd loved that about her the first time they'd been together, and now her shapely figure had his fingers itching to reach out and touch. Before he could make the move, she did so herself. Skimming her hands up her torso, she took her aroused nipples between thumbs and forefingers and rolled and pinched them.

Her moan trembled through the room, thickening the already humid air. He gulped hard, his cock pulsing with savage want. Sweat beaded on his back.

"Are you just going to stand there and watch?"

Yes. Or, shit, he should. If he were thinking at all, he would. "This is a bad idea," Brian said as he crossed the room. He couldn't stop his feet any more than his hands as he reached out and covered her fingers with his own, felt the hot press of her big nipples.

Taryn pressed her breasts against him harder as she rose to meet his mouth and nibbled at the corners of his lips. Normally, he would have four inches on her; with the heels they were almost even.

She swiped at his lips with a moist, lusty lick. "Mmm...it doesn't taste bad to me." Pressing between his lips, she sank her tongue deep, stroking at his, over his teeth, then again against his tongue. She pulled back slowly, sucking on his lips, asking in a seductive whisper, "Does it taste bad to you?"

If there was a man alive who could answer that question with a no, he wasn't in this room.

Brian pushed her hands aside and captured her breasts fully in his own hands, ran his thumbs along the stiff peaks that centered them. He wanted his tongue on her nipples, tasting, teasing. Then lower, nipping, licking, suckling at her most intimate flesh. Doing all those things he promised himself he wouldn't do. Not with her. Not ever again. "You're the devil, woman."

She smiled wickedly and brushed his lips with hers once again. "Do you want me?"

Last chance to do the right thing. "Yes." *Way to go, bucko. That wasn't even close to the right word.* Only, as Taryn had pointed out, it felt right.

She moved her hand between their bodies. Finding his erection through the slacks he changed into for dinner, she stroked the hard length. His cock jumped beneath her touch, and her smile grew salacious. "Are you going to have me?"

"God, yes." He bent his head to breast level and flicked his tongue across a swollen nipple. His body hummed as her spicy, hot flavor took over his senses and sliced tremors of ecstasy through him.

So good. So hot. So—

Taryn's laughter cut his thoughts short. Not stimulated sounding, but smug. Brian looked up to find her smile much the same. "What?" he demanded.

Lifting his hand away from her breast, she stepped back. "I was right. You said you wouldn't want me if I offered. Well, I offered, and you wanted me."

What the...? "That was a—what, a test?"

Her eyes danced with amusement. "If you need to give it a name." She pulled the top of the dress back up, snugged the zipper, and returned the straps to their places along her shoulders. "Now, excuse me, but I have a date with an island hottie. You're welcome to stay and let"—she glanced at his crotch, and her lips twitched in a way that told him she fought another laugh—"things relax. Just be gone by eleven. I'm not coming home alone, and I'm also not into threesomes."

* * *

She really shouldn't play with fire. It wasn't nice at all.

But, oh, what fun to finally get revenge against that lying jerk.

Taryn was still laughing over the stricken look on Brian's face when the island shuttle pulled up in front of the Strobe fifteen minutes later. The driver of the shuttle said the dance club served bar food, so she planned to eat something here, right after she had a victory drink.

Brian and his misplaced words had done more than scar the image she'd created of his mother. They made her, a woman who prided herself on her personal strength, feel insecure.

After finally getting over the sting of her father cutting off her college money because he didn't believe songwriting was a "real" career choice, she'd promised herself she would never doubt her abilities again. She made that same claim when she'd used the assistance of financial aid and enrolled in a songwriting course on her own, only to have the instructor tell her she wasn't cut out for it. Both times she'd gotten over her self-doubt, but with Brian it lingered on.

Tonight that lingering met its end. The insecurity was gone, and she wanted to spend the night celebrating.

And she would. Just as soon as she found the right guy to celebrate with.

Taryn moved through the crowded club and up the plankway that led toward the bar. Strobe lights the place had apparently been given its name for flickered from all directions in vivid shades of red, orange, and yellow, illuminating the otherwise dark establishment. Music blared, the base throbbing so loudly she could feel its vibrations deep within her. The club's floor was built with slanted levels, and when she reached the bar and looked down at the floor below, she could see more of most of the dancers than she ever cared to.

This place was obviously lenient with its rules, as couples, threesomes, and groups well over that number danced together on the floor, groping each other with hands above and below clothing. A redhead in the center of the floor tipped back her head. The rapturous look on the woman's face as her dance partner thrust up against her made it seem like a lot more was going on between them than dancing.

Taryn's throat went dry with the idea the two were about to fuck on the dance floor. Moist heat gathered in her sex, and her pussy pulsed as it had when she'd opened her door to find Brian standing there looking too tasty for words.

While she'd had fun toying with him, she hadn't just been playing with fire en route to revenge. Between that kiss and the few flicks of his tongue against her breast, she'd been burned. Now, she ached to be rid of the want coiled tightly in her belly. Down there, in that crush of gyrating bodies, was the place to do it.

Forgetting about a drink, Taryn moved back down the plankway and onto the teeming dance floor. She was dancing no more than half a minute before she felt someone behind her. Make that a man. A very aroused man, judging by the solid state of the cock pressing against her backside.

A large hand wrapped around her middle, settling possessively along her abdomen. The heat of his touch seeped through the thin cotton. Jolts of sensual awareness shot from her belly to her fingers and toes. He rocked into her, pressing his erection against her butt. Juices of arousal leaked from her sex to dampen her thong. Sighing over the instantaneous reaction she hadn't had over any man but Brian in far too long, she glanced down, waiting for the strobe lights to land on them. Finally, the lights came, and she nearly cried with relief when she found no ring or obvious tan line on his third finger.

Thank you. Thank you. Thank you!

She'd found her island hottie. It didn't matter if was actually hot or what size or shape he was in—though his large hand and impressive hard-on suggested he would be at least moderately tall. All that mattered was he'd managed to get her damp.

Behind her, her dance partner moved his hips against hers in a move too carnal to ignore. She thrust back against him in time with the pulsating beat of the music, and as if he took that for an invitation, he lifted her hair aside and placed his mouth on her neck. Warmth sizzled through her with the feel of his cool lips on her hot, salty flesh. The movements of their hips grew faster, falling into a unified rhythm. She could feel his solid cock against the seam of her ass now as easily as if they wore no clothes at all.

And she would have that. She would convince him to take her back to the hotel and make her balcony fantasy come true. He would fuck her so good and hard that all want for Brian would be dislodged permanently.

Her mystery lover's mouth moved farther up her neck. He nibbled on the shell of her ear, and she sucked in a breath as a shiver of excitement zipped through her. The hand on her abdomen traveled downward to rub against her mound. It should have been a move that overstepped her bounds, particularly in such a public setting. Tonight it was everything she wanted, and her shiver turned to a rapturous tremble reflected deep in her pussy.

Oh, yeah. This guy could make her forget about Brian for sure.

His lips lifted from her ear, and he asked in a rough voice, "What do you say we find a dark corner and see if we can't do something about these layers between us?"

The near-deafening club music wasn't enough to cloak the sensual invitation. "I'd say you read my mind, but a dark balcony back at my hotel room sounds even better."

Coarse facial hair brushed her ear. The hand at her crotch went from rubbing to cupping. "So you want to take me home with you, baby?"

"I do." She ground against his palm without the slightest care for who watched. Inner walls clenched, grew slicker. "I want your dick where your hand is."

"Then turn around and put it there."

Eagerness rang in his voice. Capturing his hand in hers, she spun around, smiling her fervent anticipation. And then went wide-eyed and slack jawed as disbelief clutched at her heart.

Brian. No!

But it was him standing before her. His hand she held. Brian who'd obviously followed her here to get his own revenge.

The glimmer of triumph in his eyes suggested he thought he'd gotten just that. Maybe in some ways he had. But the night was young, and she planned to be the ultimate winner before it was through.

His lips parted, and she could tell by his cocky expression he was going to comment about something, maybe the irony of the situation. Before he could get a word out, she rose up and took advantage of his open mouth by slipping her tongue inside and crushing her achingly aroused body firm to his.

Chapter Four

The feel of Taryn's lush body rubbing against his, their hips gyrating in tandem, was almost more than Brian could handle without taking things to the next level here on the Strobe's crowded dance floor. From the instant he'd spotted her, moving her dynamite curves in a way that could only be described as blatantly sexual, his dick had been rock solid. Not that it took much to reach that state.

He'd been sporting a semierection when he arrived at the dance club, thanks to her brazen behavior back at the hotel.

She'd hinted the taunting had been a test. He could guess it had been more about revenge. She had every right to be angry over his lies and the weakening effect they'd had on her confidence. He even understood her need for vengeance. What he didn't understand was her method of retaliation.

Caressing his chest, she returned her lips to his. She kissed him openmouthed, her tongue darting inward to rub against his with hot, wet, inviting strokes. Her spicy cinnamon scent reached out to his senses, enveloping him in its heady embrace. He knew better than to give in, knew he shouldn't have followed her in the first place, despite his cock's clamoring need to get inside her slick pussy. He knew it, and yet he couldn't resist.

Brian slid his hands around her waist and down to cup the plumpness of her ass. Parting her knees with one of his, he pushed his thigh between her legs and beneath the indecently short skirt of the tawdry red dress. The hardness of his leg brushed against her mound, and her tongue stilled as a hot gasp filled his mouth.

Hell, that gasp was sexy. Even nearly silenced between the press of his lips and the pulsing club music, the sensual sound stroked over his raw nerves and intensified the ache of his balls to monumental proportions.

Taryn's tongue resumed its movements. Before she could regain complete control, he took over the lead, kissing her hard and full-on, plunging his tongue deep and stroking hers with fast, meaningful thrusts. He mimicked the action with his thigh, rocking it against her sex. Warm puffs of air streamed from her nose, and she writhed her cunt against his leg deliciously each time he made contact.

If he wanted to claim revenge for the way she treated him back in her room, now was the time to do so. Pull back from her luscious mouth, tell him she failed his test, and leave her hot and wanting. Only he didn't want to leave. He wanted to revert back to his wicked thoughts when he'd first started dancing with her and fuck her right here on the dance floor, surrounded by hundreds of people, many of whom seemed to already be getting it on.

Brian licked at the hot interior of her mouth one last time and then found the spot on her neck where he'd first kissed her. He trailed his tongue the length of her salty, damp flesh, and Taryn trembled in his arms.

Nice, but not nice enough. He wanted her more than trembling. He wanted her shaking, shouting. Calling out his name as she crashed over the edge of orgasm.

Releasing a butt cheek, he brought his hand between their bodies, then down and beneath her dress. As if they were controlled by some unseen voyeur, the strobe lights returned, illuminating his hand as it disappeared beneath the cotton. Others were watching them, and while the idea of public sex hadn't crossed his mind much in the past, now it seemed a must-try event.

Each beat of the island music thundered through his veins a little faster. Taryn pumped her hips against him a little harder. The intimate press of her warm thighs against his hand sent his fingertips scurrying higher beneath her dress. She brought her hands to his neck and, without meeting his eyes, urged his mouth to the swell of her breasts.

He liked taking sex slowly, savoring it and every inch of the woman he was with. But now, with his dick aching for release and his blood sizzling with lust, he didn't want to move slowly. That she wanted only fast and furious seemed a given. Without hesitation, Brian slid his hand up her thigh until he encountered the lace of her thong. The material was drenched. Not a surprise, but still a pleasure, one that made his cock jump against his zipper. Fingering her would be good. Fucking her, here and now, would be mind-blowing.

The hold Taryn had on his neck intensified as he pushed his fingers beneath the cotton and found a pleasingly tight, wet nest of curls. That hold grew almost painful as he kissed the naked tops of her perspiration-moistened breasts and dipped a finger inside her body. And when he added a second finger and rocked them up into her taut sheath, the pain became too much to ignore.

What the hell? Was she trying to screw him, or strangle him?

Brian lifted his mouth to look at her. Her eyes were wide, the pupils dilated. Her lips swollen from when they'd kissed.

Those swollen lips parted, and Taryn frowned. "This isn't what we agreed on."

He had to be hearing her wrong. The music distorting her words. "What?"

She shook her head and pulled back, taking the luxury of her pussy with her. "We agreed I would take you back to the hotel with me."

Yeah, they had, but that was before she even knew who he was. Besides, what the hell difference did it make where they were, so long as they were both having a good time?

Unless she wasn't having a good time.

He'd once believe she had an insecure side. Had he been right about that, despite the confident and controlling way she came off? "This doesn't excite you, doing it here, knowing people are watching, getting off at the sight of your pretty pussy gobbling up my cock?"

Taryn glanced around them, at the couples and groups dancing up against each other with wild abandon, flashing patches of bared skin and breasts and intertwined bodies, leaving little to nothing to the imagination. The heat in her eyes when she looked back assured him the environment was as big of a turn-on for her as him. "Yes, it excites me, but it's not what we agreed on. We agreed to go back to the hotel, to my balcony. That's what I want. If you don't want to give it to me anymore, fine, I'll find someone who does."

No fucking way. She couldn't be serious, only the suddenly sober note in her eyes said that she was. "You'd let someone else put out the fire I started in you?"

"If they would take me back to my balcony, yes."

Then let them, man.

He should do just that—walk away and let whatever guy she chose next give her the balcony sex she craved. Brian should, but he didn't want another man finishing this for him. He always finished what he started, damn it.

Did she? Or was she still playing some kind of twisted revenge game with him? "How do I know you're serious? How do I know this isn't your way of setting me up for another test you want to see me fail?"

Taryn surprised him by admitting, "I thought about it—I love a good challenge—but I don't want that any longer." She moved closer, leaning forward until her breasts rubbed against his chest and her lips brushed his ear. "In case you couldn't tell when you were fingering me, I want you, Brian. Why shouldn't I? We've always had the heat. It's your staying power that was the problem. You say that was a onetime thing."

He bristled at the reminder. "It *was*."

"Then take me back to my room and do me."

Wanting to set her straight on his track record of stellar sexual performance or not, Brian couldn't shake the idea she would take another man home if he said no. Any man. Just someone to get her off. "Taryn…"

She pulled back and smiled knowingly. "You've changed your mind, haven't you? I put pressure on you by bringing up your endurance issue, and now you're scared. It's okay to admit it. People are scared of all kinds of things. Admitting you have the problem is the first step toward—"

He kissed her before she could get another word out. Nibbled on her full lips, then once again sank his tongue deep. He shouldn't take her back to her room knowing any man would do. He shouldn't ache to feel her tight, warm body enveloping him. Shouldn't want her period, knowing how wrong she was for him, even for one night.

But he did want her. More so than he could ever remembering wanting a woman in his life. "I don't have a problem, Taryn." He released her lips with a savage tug. "Take me to your balcony and fuck me already."

* * *

It was exactly the way she'd imagined it.

Okay, Taryn conceded, in her fantasy she'd been wearing a black dress with a wraparound necktie and nothing beneath it, but her current attire was nearly as accessible. As Brian set her on the balcony railing, she proved it by peeling the dress's thin straps down her arms, unzipping its back, and lowering the snug red cotton to her waist.

The moon was full tonight. Its rays streamed down in a golden path, sparkling in the ocean that lapped at the sand less than twenty yards from her first-floor balcony. The moonlight worked its way on Brian, as well. Slanting over his strong features, it drew out the slight growth of his dark stubble and the lust in his eyes, turning his typically tasty appeal into a thing of drugging proportions. The way he took her in was no less lethal. His gaze slid over her, hot and heavy, lingering in just the right spots to have her sex once more seeping with desire.

His hands skimmed along her sides as a featherlight distraction that spoke to each of her nerve endings. Every inch of her body came alive with raw pleasure as he bent his head and flicked his tongue over a breeze-hardened nipple. Heady sensation shot from her nipple to the depths of her pussy, and she moaned. Then again, louder, when his fingers caressed the outer swell of her breasts and his tongue lapped at the pouting bud a second time.

He was amazing with foreplay, and now that she'd decided to sleep with him, she had no qualms about admitting it.

Taryn buried her fingers in his hair. "I love your tongue, your mouth. I swear I couldn't be any wetter than I am right now."

Brian lifted his mouth from her breast. He eyed her face for a long moment before narrowing his gaze. "This better not be another test, because I swear to God, woman, there won't be any stopping me this time."

She laughed. As she'd told him back at the club, this wasn't a test, but that she had him guessing was a thing of beauty. That feeling of insecurity, temporary as it might be, she owed him. A quick, wild preconference lay that ended with her coming, he owed her.

Using her grip on his hair, she brought his mouth back to her breast. "I'm not stopping you, Brian. I'm not stopping at all until we're both trembling with climax. Now, suck on me. Show me this deity of sexual virility you claim to be."

Humor flashed through his eyes. "Yes, ma'am," he said in a thick, teasing voice.

His tongue returned to her breast, stroking her stiff nipple with long, lazy swipes and then giving the other the same treatment. Returning to the first, he pulled the bud between his lips, bit down on the crown, and gave a hard tug. Heat coursed through her veins. The muscles of her sex tightened, quivered. Her moan of ecstasy rang out into the balmy night air.

As she'd done in her fantasy, Taryn pushed him back and slid off the railing. She worked the Lycra past her hips as gracefully as possible, considering the colossal size of the task. The cotton fell free, pooling at her feet in a shimmering puddle of red. She stepped away from the dress and opened her stance. Lust coiled thick in her belly, and the juices that filled her pussy grew with the idea she was naked aside from the miniscule thong and stilettos, while he remained fully clothed.

Brian's hot look sizzled along the length of her. "Nice. Been planning that all night?"

With some lucky guy, yes. With him, not at all.

Taryn still couldn't believe he was here, playing an active role in her balcony fantasy. Finally feeling an orgasm at his hands hadn't been what she meant when she told herself she would be the ultimate winner tonight. She also couldn't discount the good to be had from it. Sharing a quick, mutually pleasurable screw with him would set right the rest of their past. The remainder of this week, she could focus all her anxiety on the conference and putting forth the best damned display of talent ever.

Smiling, she moved back to the railing and lifted herself up on it. The thong gave her ass no coverage, and the railing was cooler than she'd imagined. She shivered, and then just like in her fantasy, Brian was there. His lips back on her breasts, kissing them, caressing them. Moving lower. His tongue coasted over her stomach to dip into her navel, and she laughed at the ticklish sensation.

That laugh turned husky as he went lower still. Pulling the skimpy lace of her thong aside, he inhaled her aroused scent with a murmur of pleasure. She trembled with the satisfied sound and the predatory way he looked upon her sex, like he wouldn't just be tasting her, but feeding off her until there wasn't a lucid part of her left.

She was ready for this fantasy to become a reality. No more waiting. No more foreplay. It was time. "Condom."

"Not yet," Brian said breathily against her damp flesh.

His thumbs parted her slit, opening her pussy for the descent of his mouth. She expected the stab of his tongue. His lips came as a gentle caress of her clit. Pleasure arced through her, nearly bowing her up on the railing, and she sucked in a hard breath with the impossible intensity of such a light touch. Another caress followed by a third, and he fitted his lips to her sex wholly. His tongue licked the length of her slit. White-hot heat careened through Taryn. Delicious tension gripped her belly, coiled, spanned outward.

She gave her head a fierce shake. Nuh-uh. No way, damn it, she was not coming like this! They were having a quick, standard, run-of-the-mill lay to move beyond their past.

"Yes," she demanded. "Now!"

Struggling to ignore the decadence of his tonguing, she reached down around him and pushed her hands into his back pockets in search of a wallet. He had to have a condom.

Her fingers met with the soft leather of his wallet. She breathed a sigh of relief when she found not one but two of the blessed items and then slid off the railing. Brian jerked back with the move, nearly toppling onto his ass in the process. His grunt told her he hadn't appreciated the way she took things over.

But soon he wouldn't care. Soon he would be buried balls-deep inside her, shaking with climax as she rode him over the edge.

She made fast work of his slacks and briefs, noting then discarding the way he stood stock-still, as if he wasn't having the time of his life. The thick, solid length of his cock when she unrolled the condom on it assured her that he was happy.

Taryn slid the dripping thong down her legs, then straightened. Blood pounded in her ears and pussy in tandem. She grinned her anticipation. "All set."

He didn't grin back. But he did look eager.

Long moments passed, him staring at her with that predatory gleam in his eyes. Finally, he said, "Then let's get busy."

Wrapping his hands around her waist, he pushed her back, all the way back against the wall and into near darkness. She thought he would use the wall for support, lift her up around his waist, and impale her on his dick, give them both what they craved. Instead, he lowered to his knees and kissed her inner thigh.

Impatience furled through her. What the hell?

She was ready to go off like a bottle rocket, and he was slowing things down. "Brian?"

He didn't respond, just kept nibbling his way up her leg.

"Don't you think we're past that? I'm ready. I'm wet. I'm horny. I want your cock buried inside me. Now!"

Still, he nibbled, rubbing his stubble against her thigh and sending tingles of excitement dancing through her body. She didn't know such a thing was possible, but she grew all the wetter, all the hungrier, all the more ready to burst.

Too ready.

"Time's up." Taryn bent to his level, took hold of his shoulders, and pounced.

She missed her target. They landed with a shared *oomph* on the balcony, his back against the concrete, her lying lengthwise over him. She meant to land like this, but with a certain part of him buried in a certain part of her. She corrected that now, taking his cock in hand and aligning it with her sex.

She sat back and cried out at the electric sensation as she slid down his length. It had been way too long since she'd gotten laid. Days. Weeks. Months. Hell, right now it felt like decades. Maybe that was why she couldn't sit still. She had to move. Fast.

Brian reached up and captured her breasts, loved the throbbing nipples with his fingertips slowly even as the rest of him gave in to her hasty tempo. For a half minute it was all good, all great, all freaking incredible, and then he stopped moving.

"Son of a bitch, Taryn. If you don't slow down, you're going to regret it."

"I can't." Salacious tremors shook through her belly. Zings of pleasure quaked in her pussy. She was so close... "Besides, you don't want me to."

"Yes, I do," he said through gritted teeth. "It's been a while, Taryn. Slow down."

"No." She couldn't slow down. It might have been a while for him, but it was clearly longer for her, because she could *not* stop. She had to reach the end. Climax was building inside her to the breaking point. An inferno flamed in her belly; cream dribbled from her sex.

Just a few more seconds. Just the right angle...

Grabbing hold of Brian's forearms, she leaned forward and rocked against him harder, felt the hard scrape of his pubic bone against her engorged clit. A dizzy rush of almost-there sensations spirited through her. And then quickly on the tail of those another sensation, that of Brian tensing beneath her, his body bowing up and then jerking in telltale fashion. A grimace stole over his features. Next came the hot push of cum filling the condom.

Disbelief shook Taryn to the core. No, he did not! But he had. He *had*.

Every inkling of arousal evaporated, jetting her from *almost there* to *why the hell did I let him take me there* in the space of a heartbeat.

His grimace turned to a scowl. "Goddamn—I told you to slow down!"

"You ruined it. I can't believe you ruined it." She couldn't believe she was still on his lap either. Quickly, she rose to her feet and turned away.

"What did I ruin?" he asked, not sounding the slightest bit sympathetic.

"My balcony fantasy. It was going to be so good, and you ruined it with your speedy little friend."

"He isn't so little."

She heard the contempt in his voice and smiled. "At least you aren't singing that 'he isn't so speedy' song anymore."

"He isn't so speedy, either, damn it." Brian's hand came around her forearm, and he swiveled her back to face him. From the tight set of his lips to his accusing eyes, he didn't look happy. "This is *your* fault. I told you to stop. I told you that if you didn't slow down, this would happen. I told you it had been a while. But *you* wouldn't listen." He let go of her arm to point a finger at her. "*You* are the one who ruined your balcony fantasy. Not me. You are an aggressive, sexual control freak."

Better a control freak than a total prick on an ego redemption trip. Only, she was no control freak.

Taryn turned her own finger on him, jabbing it into his gut. "I am *not* a sexual control freak! But you...you, mister, are nasty. Every time your ego takes a hit, you have to turn it around and make someone else feel bad. I am done feeling bad because of you."

Letting his hand fall back at his side, Brian expelled a long breath of air. "I'm not trying to make you feel bad, Taryn. I'm telling you the truth. If you just let me call the shots for a while, the night doesn't have to be over. I can get hard again fast. Until then, let me make you come. I swear you won't regret it."

Yeah, right. As if she would believe anything he had to say. She'd made that mistake one too many times and look where it had gotten her. "I don't want you and Quick to the finish Willy in my room a second longer."

His grimace returned. "I'll admit to being at fault five years ago, but not this time. I haven't gotten laid in a while, but even if I had, I wouldn't have been able to hold off much longer the way you were pushing me. No man could."

"Other men have."

"How long—five minutes? Ten tops?"

"I have one word for you, Brian. Viagra."

Taryn jerked his clothes off the balcony and stalked inside the hotel room. Brian followed with an appalled snort, and she thrust the clothes into his arms and jerked her chin toward the door. "You have thirty seconds to be dressed and out that door. After that, I'm calling security and letting them haul your sorry naked ass away."

Chapter Five

He was *so* full of it!

Aggressive, Taryn would own up to—that was just because she knew what she liked. But a sexual control freak? *I think not.*

What Brian said about other men not being able to last around her, he couldn't be more wrong about that. She'd been with plenty of men who had lasted a long, long time, and they'd both gotten off before the fun was over with, thank you very much.

Of course, most of that long, long time happened before the guy was actually inside her and, yeah, she generally only came when she was on top and making sure the right spots were hit, but come on, she was *not* a sexual control freak.

She wasn't. Nuh-uh.

Her chin quivered. She plopped down on the bed, fighting off tears of frustration.

Damn it, she did not like that man.

He messed with her head. Made her want him. Made her ache for him. Then when he finally had her, he saw to his own happiness and, meanwhile, played on her insecurities.

Taryn gasped. She had said good-bye to her insecurities the moment she left this room with Brian in it. They would not come back because of him and his control problems. She was good in bed. Damn good. And she could prove it too.

Picking up the phone, she jabbed in Sarah's number.

The phone rang twice, and then a sleepy female voice said, "Hell—"

"You'd better say hell. You are in *such* big trouble."

"Taryn?"

"This is all *your* fault. I told you I needed you along with me. I told you I wouldn't be able to handle it without you. That I'd fall off the deep end and sleep with him the first chance I got."

Sarah seemed to come awake then, as her laughter spilled through the phone line. "Those weren't your exact words, and whoever he is, you would have slept with him whether I was there or not. In fact, if I were there, we both would have found ourselves a man to keep us occupied for the week. We're sexually aggressive women who know what we want and go after it, Tare. That's not a bad thing."

Sexually aggressive? "Tell me you did *not* just say that. I suppose you think we're both control freaks too."

There was a pause, then, "I'm not."

Pauses did not lie. But clearly her so-called best friend was trying to. "But I am? You think I'm a control freak, and you somehow failed to mention this even once in the four years we've been friends?"

"I didn't say you were a control freak, Taryn. It's…" Another pause. "It's almost two in the morning here. I was half-asleep when I answered."

Half-asleep? Taryn was in the middle of a crisis, and *that* was the only excuse Sarah could come up with? "You are *so* not the best friend I thought you were."

The subtle creak of a mattress drifted through the receiver followed by Sarah's sigh. "Chill out. I don't think you're a control freak. But I do think you are totally freaking out. Who did you sleep with, and where is he now?"

"Brian. That's who I slept with. And I have no idea where he is, because I kicked him out after he gave a repeat performance of last time." How could she ever have believed his "it was a onetime thing" spiel? He wasn't a man to be trusted. He ate poor, suffering businesspeople for breakfast and used the profit from the sale of their companies to buy his dinner for goodness' sake.

"Oh," Sarah said, no longer sounding even remotely amused.

That was the friend Taryn knew, wallowing right alongside her. "Yeah, oh. He not only ruined my balcony fantasy, but he told me I'm an aggressive, sexual control freak. That's why he can't ever keep from blowing it early around me. I am not a control freak, and you know it, don't you?"

"Well, I've never slept with you, so I'm not the best judge, but I don't think that's true. He was probably just feeling—"

"Like his precious ego took another beating. That's what I said. I was right. I knew I was, but hearing you agree makes me feel a lot better." She knew she'd done the right thing by calling. This emotional, and admittedly somewhat flaky, eruption was the kind of thing only a true friend could understand. The man just drove her nuts, made her act and feel like she had more than a few screws loose. "Thanks. You really are an awesome friend. Talk to you soon."

Taryn replaced the phone and let out a breath, feeling both saner and free of the insecurities Brian managed to dredge up. The unencumbered feeling lasted long enough for her to get ready for bed and lie down. The second her head hit the pillow, the insecurity returned, eating away at her restless mind like a living, breathing evil thing.

If he'd attacked her songwriting abilities again, she could have ignored it or at least tried to. While he might be a sponsor for this conference, he wasn't an expert on music of any kind. But he hadn't attacked her songwriting abilities. He'd attacked her as a woman. And given he wasn't just playing at being someone who understood what a man liked, but actually was a man and ought to know as well as the rest of the male population, that hurt.

Taryn flopped onto her belly and plumped up her pillow, sank her head back down, and closed her eyes. She counted to a hundred. Then two hundred. Then counted images of herself strangling Brian. Still, she didn't sleep.

Obviously, she wouldn't be sleeping at all tonight. Or anytime in the foreseeable future, so long as self-doubt roamed about in her mind taking potshots at her sound logic. And that meant she had only one option.

She had to find a place nearby—a restaurant, a deli, a gas station, anywhere—that carried quality ice cream and proceed to gorge herself on Chocolate Cashew Heaven.

* * *

The last thing Taryn suffered from was insecurity of any kind. What better way of proving her confidence than spending the afternoon baking in the tropical sun wearing nothing more than her tanning oil and shades?

Her belly roiled as she stepped out of her shorts and set them on the foot of the beach towel she'd laid out. Lack of self-assurance was not to blame for the uneasy sensation, just lack of prior exposure. She'd sunbathed topless plenty of times back in Michigan during the peak summer months, but she'd never bared her bottom half to the bulk of humanity during the daylight hours.

Okay, so by the looks of most of the beachgoers, not the bulk of humanity, rather the bulk of the folks from the island's senior center.

A bald man who looked in his seventies, quickly edging toward eighty, stood from a lawn chair thirty feet away and headed in the direction of the rising surf. Taryn cringed at his saggy, white backside view. Taking in the scenery was *not* a good idea.

Maybe that most of the strangers were old enough to be grandparents was the real reason she felt apprehensive about stripping. The important things were that they weren't her grandparents and that she was not insecure.

She also wasn't an aggressive, sexual control freak.

Taryn lay on the beach towel, pulled the T-shirt over her head, and unhooked her bikini top. That Brian's obnoxious words were still in her mind could only be blamed on this island's lack of amenities. She scrounged every open shop she could find last night and discovered not one of them carried Chocolate Cashew Heaven. That meant not only hadn't she slept worth a damn, but she would be miserable and without a cure for the rest of the week.

Only, no, she was not going to be miserable.

She was going to be naked. And glistening brown. And tonight...tonight she would find herself a real island hottie who had neither a problem with staying power nor ensuring his ego stayed intact by being nasty to those he felt threatened it.

With a last look around to see if anyone was staring in her direction, Taryn set her bikini top aside and squirmed out of the bottoms. Grabbing her MP3 player from the beach bag, she scanned to one of her demo songs and put on her headphones. Eyes closed, she pictured herself surrounded by bronzed island gods, all of whom were vying for the chance to spend the night worshipping at her temple, because as lovers went, she wasn't a control freak at all, but a model of sexual equality and goodness.

* * *

"What are you listening to?"

Brian managed to hold in his laughter over the look of disgust on Taryn's face. If the sound found its way out, it would be a rock-solid, rough-edged giveaway to the equally solid state of his dick.

The brunette who worked the Seaside's registration desk and seemed to be Taryn's supplier for island information had been a little too forthcoming on Taryn's whereabouts. Almost as if the girl knew how equally anxious and stoked he'd be to learn Taryn was headed to a nude beach. He stood over Taryn now, struggling his damnedest to keep his cock from tenting the front of his swim trunks. The jet-black of her hair made for a killer contrast against the pallor of her skin. It took too damned much self-control not to dive down on the towel and join her for a literal tumble in the sand.

She sat up, jerking off her sunglasses. Her big breasts jiggled tauntingly. Coconut mingled with the briny ocean air to work a number on his already hyperaware senses. A drop of oil slipped from her shoulder with her ascent. The tiny pearl of moisture trickled between the lush valley of her breasts and continued on a downward path way in the hell too dangerous to follow.

Taryn narrowed her eyes. "None of your business..." She seemed to catch on to the fact he was having a hard time staying focused on her face then and followed his wandering gaze. A mingling of shock and understanding slipped through her eyes. She sent her discarded clothes a wary look.

He didn't want her putting them back on. For one thing, she had a gorgeous body—as he was sure all the old geezers on the beach had noticed—and absolutely nothing to be ashamed of. For another thing, it was clear she only wanted them on to keep her body from him.

When Brian had set out to find Taryn, it had been in an attempt to apologize for his behavior last night. Not that he thought he'd been in the wrong with his accusation over her controlling personality, or the one responsible for ruining her balcony fantasy, but at the same time, he'd clearly hurt her again. He didn't want that between them. He didn't want a single thing between them from this point onward.

No, as he watched her rosy nipples pucker under the heat of his gaze, he didn't want a single thing between them at all. Just skin on skin. Flesh slapping sweat-moistened flesh. Hungry mouth devouring hungry mouth. Warm, swollen breasts. Lower to lap at her sweet, salty feminine lips, deep into her creamy—

"You can stop mentally fucking me anytime."

He wished he could. He'd tracked her down to clear the air, but now he didn't want it clear. Now he ached for one more chance to prove that Quick to the finish Willy, as she'd called his dick, wasn't quick in the least, or for that matter named Willy.

In dire need of a diversion, Brian grabbed the headphones from her head and put them on.

"Hey!" Taryn yelped, but made no move to stand. Probably because she realized doing so would put on full display the few parts of her he'd yet to see in the daylight.

Ah, but he'd felt those parts. Tasted those parts.

The song bleeding through the headphones, or rather the familiar soft, throaty voice, stifled the thought. "Is this you?"

"Yes." She extended a hand, palm-side up. "Now, give them back. I've already had more than enough of your opinions for one lifetime."

"You have a good voice." It was a fact, not a compliment.

Her glare lightened up. "Thanks. But I'm not a singer." She cast a surreptitious glance around, then asked, "Do you like the song?"

Astonishment sliced through him. After last night, Brian never would have believed she'd cared for his opinion enough to bother asking. He wanted to answer her with an indubitable yes, but he refused to lie. Even if it destroyed any chance he had of proving his sexual prowess, he had no choice but to be honest.

Unless she didn't want honesty. "Do you want my honest answer, or the yes your family and friends give you?"

Something flickered through her eyes—annoyance, possibly—and he thought she would tell him not to bother with an answer, or maybe to get screwed. Then she said, "I want honesty."

"It's nice."

Dejection flared in her eyes. Irritation masked it as she pulled her lips into a snarl. "Nice?" she retorted. "That's it? Just *nice*?"

Believing her anger would be the easy way out. Yesterday afternoon, even last night, when she'd thrown him out of her hotel room, he would have believed it. Now, he felt her initial sadness was closer to the truth.

Compassion pulled at his gut. He knew exactly how hard it was to make it in this industry. Could imagine how much time, effort and, no doubt, money she'd already put forth. He still wasn't taking his words back. "You said you wanted honesty, Taryn. It's a good song. But it's not a great song. Something's missing."

Her cheeks pinked. She shot to her feet and made a jumping grab for the headphones. Repeating the move when he blocked her attempts the first time, she bit out, "What would you know about it? You're a businessman."

"That might be, but I also grew up listening to my mother practice her songs for hours on end, not to mention helped her write several of them."

Taryn stopped jumping. Hands on her hips, she frowned. "Not that I'm saying I trust your opinion—because frankly there's very little chance I do—but what do you think is missing?"

Brian felt like the better half of his brain was missing at the moment, with her standing there, breasts thrust forward and her stance wide-open. Her pussy would be open as well, lips parted invitingly, the fine wisps of pubic hair no match for their plumpness.

His cock jerked hard against his shorts, and he bit back a grunt.

Fuck, he had to focus. For whatever reason, Taryn was giving him a chance to redeem himself. While he still didn't think he had any real reason to seek

redemption from her, there wasn't any knocking the
idea she would like him a whole better and, therefore,
be a whole lot more open to the idea of letting him back
into her bed, if he helped her. Then there was the
simple fact he liked helping people.

It was a trait passed down from his mother that
he rarely had the chance to let show. He'd learned the
hard way helping, and, in doing so, opening himself up
to others had a way of ending painfully. He could help
Taryn without having to worry over either pain or
getting too close. They would be inhabiting the same
hotel for the week, seeing each other for the sake of the
conference. After that, they would be hundreds of miles
apart. Getting an invitation to this conference was a
onetime deal for her, and the rest of the year he was
rarely involved with the music industry, which meant
they would be moving in circles that couldn't be further
apart.

"Passion," Brian finally said, wishing it weren't so
easy to identify. Any other lone element would be
moderately easy to fix. Passion had to come from the
heart. "The words are there, but not enough to make
me believe them. If I don't believe them, I won't want
to buy the song."

Taryn's lips parted far enough to show her
surprise. Her eyes narrowed after a moment, and she
shook her head. "You're wrong. It's not passion. It can't
be, because my songwriting career is the thing I'm
most passionate about in this world. Listen again."

"It *is* passion." He took the headphones off and
placed them on her head. "*You* listen. Not as the

composer, but as a buyer. Do you feel like the song's about the person who wrote it?"

She frowned. "It's not supposed to be about me."

"That's a problem, because it has to be. What makes a song sail to the top of the charts is that the buyer can both relate to the words and either sympathize for or celebrate with the singer, because it seems like they're going through whatever they're singing about. You might not be a singer, but it's your job as the songwriter to get quality music in the singer's hands."

Her frown deepened, eyebrows drawing together. "Oh."

Gone was the irritation of seconds ago. She looked sorrowful now, in a way that Brian had never seen on her. Once again he found himself wondering over the woman beneath the typically confident outer shell. If the face she showed him now was any sign, Taryn had an insecure side to her for certain. An insecurity he could potentially help lessen. "Is the song I listened to the one you were planning to use for Saturday's showcase performance?"

"It's my best. At least," she added softly, "I thought it was."

"There's still time to get the passion into it. It won't take much, a few tweaks here and there." An understatement by far, but she needed to hear it. She had to get that vulnerable look off her face. Before he pulled her into his arms for a hug that started as comfort and ended with him taking her right there in the sand. "I can help."

A disbelieving smile flirted with her lips. "Wouldn't that be considered cheating?"

Since he was sitting out judging this year, not to any great extent and certainly not more so than sleeping with him would be. "It could make a wave or two if someone found out, I suppose. I know I wouldn't tell them."

"Why would you want to help? You're hardly the type who does things out of the goodness of his heart."

Ouch. "When exactly did you make this astute decision about me?"

"I didn't have to; it's obvious. Everything I've ever read about you or heard said talked about what a cutthroat businessman you are. The antithesis of Robin Hood. You steal from the soon-to-be poor and give to yourself."

Brian couldn't stop his laughter. It was miracle she'd ever given him a second chance at sex. His laughter died down as it occurred to him she'd been keeping tabs on him these last five years. He stored that information away for later. "I hate to break it to you, but not everything you read in a magazine or hear on the radio, or wherever it is you're hearing all this stuff about me, is accurate. Some of it couldn't be further from the truth."

She looked skeptical. "You honestly want to help me out just because? There isn't a single thing in it for you?"

"It would seem that way... Unless, I was using reverse psychology and offering to help you in the hopes of getting close enough to talk you into giving submissive sex a try."

She grimaced. "I'm *not* a sexual control freak."

"Maybe not." She also hadn't said no to his idea, which left room for possibilities. Possibilities, now that it was clear she didn't hate him for admitting the truth about her music, he allowed himself to consider in detail by letting his gaze roam the length of her.

Sometime during the conversation her nipples had ceased their standing show. Under his perusal, they returned to their erect state, firming big and hard atop her beautiful breasts. He dared to move lower, to the hedonistic bounty between her thighs. His groan was guttural and overt at the sight of her freshly shaven mound. The slightly parted display of her pussy lips had him ready to go down on his knees there in the sand and devour her cunt.

Taryn squirmed. A too-damned-sexy whimper left her lips. He forced his gaze back to hers. This was a nude beach, not a brothel, and it would be wise for his raging dick to remember that. "Think about what I said, about helping you out. In the meantime..." He nodded to a volleyball net set up some thirty yards down the beach. Beachgoers were slowly making their way over to start a game. "What do you say to a little volleyball? I'll show you what a helpful guy I am and do everything in my power to let your team win."

Taryn glanced at the net, the dozen or so naked players, and then back at him. Challenge gleamed in her eyes. "I'd say I don't need that kind of help, and you're overdressed."

"Are you asking me to take my clothes off?"

She looked down at his groin, to where his cock was giving a very obvious salute, and her smile turned naughty. "Yeah, and for once see if you can keep your friend in check longer than the minute it takes to get him naked."

Chapter Six

It took almost more strength than Taryn had to drag herself to the hotel room door and answer the knock. The only reason she finally got up from bed and went to the door was because she heard Brian call her name.

They'd played several matches of volleyball, and her team had won all but the last one. That match she lost for them because she'd been doing some sightseeing at the time. It hadn't been of an island hottie, either, but of the hottie on the other side of the net who was coming off as a completely different man than what she led herself to believe the last five years. Brian was still lacking in the sack—he could claim to the contrary all he wanted, she wasn't buying it—but maybe they could be friends. Friends who grew physically aroused whenever they were within twenty feet of each other.

Okay, so maybe not friends, but maybe something.

Taryn opened the door to see his sexy, smiling face. Despite her bodily misery, her sex contracted on a famished pang of wanting. Yeah, they could never be just friends.

"Hi," she murmured. Even that took too much effort.

His smile vanished. "You look...not so good."

"I hurt. Bad. Really bad." She stepped back into the room. When he followed her inside and closed the door, she slowly returned to the bed and lay down, whimpering when her back hit the mattress.

"You're burned," he said needlessly, considering the only part of her not lobster red was the skin around her eyes because she'd worn her sunglasses the bulk of the afternoon.

Quite the pair they were. Her Rocky Raccoon. Him Speedy Gonzales. An odd couple for certain. "I'm fried. Toasted. Overcooked."

Brian's face appeared above her. "You put on sunscreen, right?"

He looked concerned. It was unexpected and yet nice. She found herself smiling, actually more like grimacing; it was all she could manage. "Oil."

"But not sunscreen?"

Her smile fled. She'd been an idiot. She knew all the risks, knew how important sunscreen was. Just... "I meant to. I had it in my bag. But then you showed up and distracted me. And...it's your fault."

"Isn't everything my fault around you?"

Most of it, yes. And in a way this was too. It was her own fault for not putting on sunscreen when she first arrived at the beach, but his fault for her not putting it on after he'd arrived and started being nice to her. He acted as though he was interested in her songwriting, in seeing her give her best effort during the showcase performance. So few others in her life had shown even that much interest, and so while he might not have said her music was great, he'd made her feel something other than loathing toward him.

Taryn wasn't admitting that.

She would take the blame, though. "It's not your fault. It's my own, and I can't fix it. I can hardly stand to move. I look like a deep-fried lobster, and there isn't even any damned Chocolate Cashew Heaven on this island."

"What?"

"Ice cream. I need ice cream."

Brian's lips quirked into the addictively yummy smile, and her belly did a slow roll. "You need aloe. Several quarts of it, if the rest of you looks like your arms, legs, and face."

"It doesn't." Taryn forgot all about his smile and winced at the memory of trying to ease her ache earlier. "It's worse. I'm itchy all over. I scratched my nipple so hard a while ago, I thought it would fall off."

"Ouch. Do you think maybe I should check it out to make sure you didn't do any permanent damage?" Amusement lit his eyes.

She laughed at his obvious attempt to make her feel better, then winced again as a shudder of pain racked through her.

The humor left his expression. "I came to see if you wanted to get some dinner, but I'm guessing that would be a no, so do you want me to bring some dinner up here for you?"

"Is this another of your 'I want to do it because I like to help people' things?"

A fresh smile curved his lips. "If it will make you say yes, then yeah, it is. I have aloe in my room. I'll bring it back with the food."

"All right. I don't think I could handle going downstairs right now, let alone having all those moms pointing me out as an example of a dumb thing to do to their kids. Dinner and aloe in my room sound great."

* * *

"Take off your clothes and roll over."

"What?" Taryn gasped.

Brian had wanted to speak the words since this afternoon when she'd put her clothes back on before leaving the beach. Only, he'd wanted to say them when he could do something about it. Right now, he would be lucky to touch her without hurting her.

He set the bottle of aloe on the end table and sank down on the edge of the bed. "You can't reach your back or a good part of the rest of your body, so I'm going to put the aloe on for you. Come on. I've seen everything you have several times, not to mention touched most of it. Strip already. Or I can do it for you, if you need help."

"I can do it." She pushed up on her elbows, puffed out a breath, and fell back on the bed. "Help. Please."

The burn didn't look so bad as to need medical attention, but then it didn't look like much fun either. And, knowing Taryn, she wouldn't give in and let him undress her unless she was feeling awful.

Brian moved to the end of the bed, straddled her legs, and pulled her toward him. She whimpered as he slipped her T-shirt over each arm and then her head. She wore no bra beneath. Her chest obviously didn't get much sun exposure, because it appeared a darker red than the rest of her.

Or so he thought until he removed her shorts and panties. Talk about burned.

"You are not to leave this hotel room the rest of the week without sunscreen on. SPF 60." Taryn made some quiet noises he took to be agreement. He finished undressing her and helped her roll over onto her stomach. "All done. Relax, and I'll put the aloe on you."

"I feel like an invalid."

She didn't look like an invalid from this angle. Even red and achy, she looked better than any other woman he could remember being with. That she was a real woman had to be what did it for him. She had a real waist, real hips. A really nice ass he had the sudden urge to swat. Later. Right now she would find no pleasure in that sort of sensual pain.

Grabbing the aloe bottle, Brian returned to the bed and straddled her upper thighs. He squeezed a generous amount of aloe onto his hands and then placed them on Taryn's back. Her skin was so hot to touch. She was so hot...

"Ew. Ow. Ohhh..."

And those moans weren't helping him to forget that fact. Especially that last one, where the cooling effect of the aloe had clearly sunk in. He wished he'd gotten dressed for this evening's conference meeting before returning to Taryn. As it was, he wore his swim trunks and his cock was growing fast against the flimsy inner seam, eager for a way out. "Better?"

"Cold. Soothing. Good."

He applied more aloe, letting it sink in, and then ran his hands the length of her back.

"Mmm...yummy..."

Yummy? So much for keeping his mind off sex.

He couldn't get to all of her breasts from this angle, but he filled his palms with more aloe and reached beneath her to massage as much of the generous globes as he could reach. His thumbs grazed the edge of her nipples, and she jerked beneath him. "Does that hurt?"

"No. It's..." Her voice was sleepy and droned off as he ran his thumbs in lazy circles over the outer edges of her breasts and then massaged them along her sides. Almost soundlessly, she asked, "What are you doing?"

Sporting some major wood.

He loved caressing women's bodies, getting to know each curve, every angle. Taryn had never let him near hers long enough to explore. Now, she was at his mercy, and he wanted to touch every inch of her, feel her come alive beneath his fingertips. Trace the indent of her spine all the way to the hollow just about her ass.

"You're tense." Brian applied more aloe. Splaying his hands over her back, he ran them down to the base of her spine. He dipped his thumbs into the shallow, drawing them back and forth across the sensitive flesh. She drew taut beneath him, and he smiled. "I'm working out the tension when the aloe has your body cooled down enough to touch. Do you want me to stop?"

"No. It's okay. You can keep going."

Even sleepy, he caught the hint of a command in Taryn's words. He grinned. "You're giving me permission to keep giving you a massage. How generous."

This time she stiffened beneath him for real. "You asked if I wanted you to stop. I never said you had to start in the first place."

"Relax, Taryn," he said soothingly, rubbing his knuckles along her shoulder blades while bending his head. "I want to do this. You have extremely soft skin. I like touching it." He dropped his mouth on the center of her back and this time used his tongue to cool her heated flesh. "I like tasting it more." He stroked her with several long, slow licks that cost his body dearly, and then drew back. "But I know you don't like that. You're not into taking the time to taste, are you? You like it fast, hard. Rough."

"I don't always like it that way," she admitted, her voice low, husky, her breathing intensifying along with his own.

"When don't you like it that way?"

Right now.

The words seemed to hang between them. Finally, she said, "Sometimes."

"Sometimes I like it fast, hard, and rough too. But I like those times better when I'm the one in control, or at least when I know it's going to be intense."

He shouldn't make this a sexual event, at least not more so than what Taryn's throaty sighs and moans were doing. Yet Brian couldn't stop his fingers from continuing their journey down her back, along the cleft of her buttocks and into the hollow between her thighs.

He found her clit swollen and stroked it. "Man, how'd I miss this knot? It's huge."

Taryn's hips bucked beneath him as he coaxed the bundle of nerves with his fingertip. He picked up the pace, applying more pressure until she whimpered.

He lowered his chest to her back, careful not to put much weight on her tender body. He breathed hotly in her ear. "Tight."

He slipped a finger into her soft, hairless opening from behind, and she sighed out a, "Yesss…"

"Wet." He added a second finger.

He ran his chin along the side of her neck, remembering how she responded to the short scruff he could never keep away longer than five or six hours at a time. Many days he hated it. Today, knowing how effectively the whiskers heightened her arousal, wasn't one of those days.

Taryn's dampening pussy contracted around his fingers. Her rapid breathing was music to his ears, ripe to the max with passion.

"Wet. Good. More. Now." The last word sounded as demand, and she ordered, "Make me come."

Brian laughed to himself. How could she seriously believe she wasn't a sexual control freak?

He'd prove to her how good being submissive could feel. Just as soon as she was feeling more like Taryn the confident and less a lobster in the boiling pot.

For now, he gave her what she craved. Catching her ear in the gentle nibble of his teeth, he thrust his fingers into her sheath. With each stroke, he brushed her clit. With each pump, he worked her earlobe. Within a minute, she gave him his reward. The muscles of her sex tightened, tensed, and then finally clamped down around him, tugging at his fingers while she coated them with her silky cream.

"Chocolate Cashew Heaven," Taryn said languidly.

Brian wondered over the words, but dismissed them to ask, "Is your sunburn better?"

"Better. Think I'm floating."

He wished he could stay here and show her how close to heaven he could take her. Business had to come first. After giving her neck a final nibble, he stood and adjusted his painfully stiff cock. Now came the part where he hobbled back to his room and got his body under control so he could see to conference business. "When you come down from that cloud, your dinner's on the table. And dessert."

"Wait!" The lethargy was gone from Taryn's voice. She pushed up on her elbows to look at him and only cringed a little with the movement. "Where are you going? I thought you were having dinner with me."

"I'd planned to, want to, but between waiting for dinner to be cooked and then the massage, I'm out of time. I have a preconference meeting at seven thirty.

Mostly it's an excuse for the committee members to run up a high bar tab and charge it to the conference, but I'm expected to be there."

"Oh. Well, then...have a good night. I guess I'll see you around."

The dejected look—the one from the beach that made him wonder who she really was—had returned. Brian wanted to go to her and show her how badly he didn't want to leave. But he really did have to be at this meeting.

They still had six days. That was plenty of time to prove what a skilled lover he was, and in turn, show her it was okay to let go of control once in a while. Tonight was a good start. Tomorrow would be even better.

"You'll see me around, Taryn, and remember what I said about helping you to find your passion. I wrote my room number down next to the phone. Any time you decide you want to take me up on the offer, stop by, and I guarantee you we'll find passion."

Chapter Seven

Taryn wanted to be mad with Brian for taking advantage of her weakened state of mind and body. But that was hard to do when he'd brought her Chocolate Cashew Heaven. She had no idea where he found it on the island, but after gobbling up the mouthwatering seafood fettuccine he'd left on the sitting area table, she'd eaten the entire pint of ice cream in fifteen minutes flat.

Between the overdose of sun, the orgasmic massage, the carb-rich dinner, and then the ice cream, she'd fallen asleep shortly after eight. She'd woken this morning to find moving was no longer a lesson in pain tolerance, and that, while her nose and cheeks were still quite pink, the rest of her looked decidedly more tan than red. Even the raccoon effect was lessening.

Thank God too. She had no longing to start out this conference looking like the woman not intelligent enough to use sunscreen.

The conference would kick off this evening with dinner, a welcome from the conference chair, and an icebreaker session. She didn't know what the icebreaker would entail, but ice of any kind sounded good to her overheated body. The red might be slowly fading, but heat still consumed her.

Not the electrifying kind of heat Taryn experienced last night at Brian's amazingly astute hands either.

For a guy who couldn't hold off his climaxes longer than a couple of minutes, he'd done a damned fine job of getting her off without seeming the least bit concerned about himself. Unless that had been the real reason he'd taken off so soon: to go back to his hotel room for a premeeting masturbation session.

The thought was meant to make her smile, not conjure up an image of him doing just that. Still, the vision filled her head. One of Brian standing naked in the shower, his cock tight in his fist while steaming hot water pounded down around him. His muscles would tighten, his balls would throb, his features would grow taut as his hand worked up and down the length of his erection. The growl escaping his mouth as he came would be primal, needy. A sound of complete surrender to the desire erupting between his thighs.

Heat licked through Taryn's body. She shook her head. She had to get out of this room, with its forbidden memories of Brian making her come so fast and hard, she'd actually compared the explosion that rocked her to the core to Chocolate Cashew Heaven. Had actually come close to a cardinal sin when she considered the orgasm might just have been better than her favorite ice cream.

Yeah, she had to find something else to occupy her thoughts, something constructive and about anything or anyone but Brian.

Comforted by the idea, Taryn grabbed her beach bag. She deposited a paperback, water bottle, beach towel, and SPF 30 sunscreen inside the bag, and headed for the door.

Twenty minutes later, she'd found a palm tree-shaded spot on one of the island's many white sand beaches—this one not a nude beach populated by grandparents. This beach appeared dedicated to the twenty- and thirtysomething couple set. The idea she was one of the few people on the beach without a partner unnerved her a little. Maybe this *was* a couple's beach. Finding another shady spot on a different beach wouldn't take long and was bound to be more relaxing.

Taryn started to gather the items she'd taken out of her bag when voices off to the right stopped her. The couple was hidden from the view of anyone lying in the sun by the ascending ridge of a sand dune. Taryn wasn't lying in the sun, and her view of the pair couldn't be more unobstructed.

A dark-haired man lay on a blanket with his snake-tattooed back facing Taryn. A woman was on the blanket beside him, the only sign of her existence an arm draped around Snake Guy's waist. An arm, and her laughter. They were both laughing. Not normal laughter, but intimate laughter. The kind that proceeded—yep—moans.

A tanned leg wrapped around Snake Guy's thigh, sliding up and down the length exposed beneath his black swim trunks. With a rough chuckle, he pushed up on an elbow and rolled over and on top of the woman, who Taryn could now see was a petite brunette with small bare breasts. She wore only blue bikini bottoms, which were soon stripped away by way of Snake Guy's mouth.

Moving down her body, he caught the side string of the bottoms in his teeth and pulled them down her legs. He took her ankles in his hands and pushed her knees up, exposing a slim patch of dark pubic curls that revealed more of her sex than they concealed. With a quick, teasing look at the brunette's face, he buried his head between her thighs. The woman's hands pushed into the guy's hair. Her hips bucked against his feasting lips, and a barely audible whimper escaped her mouth that was a carbon copy of Taryn's own.

Taryn squirmed as heat charged through her body. Her pussy convulsed, and her own bikini bottoms grew damp with her juices. She fought the urge to keep watching. It was wrong to be a voyeur to the actions of two lovers who had no idea she was ogling them. She sure as heck wouldn't want anyone spying on her when she was having sex.

Okay, she might. She'd been more than a little aroused by the thought of that very thing the night before last at the Strobe with Brian.

Brian.

If he were here right now, maybe she would be the naked one, the one sighing her building need as he tongued her hot, wet body.

And maybe she should get the hell out of here. Not only did Taryn suddenly feel like a pervert, but she was fantasizing about Brian. Sex with Brian was not good. No matter what he might claim, no matter how accomplished he was at finger fucking, it wouldn't be good, and it also wouldn't be happening ever again.

Like it or not, she wouldn't be having sex with anyone during this week away from the mundane. The conference would start in a few hours, and that meant the time for pleasure had passed, and business was about to begin.

* * *

The welcome dinner was the perfect way for Taryn to get her mind back on business. The banquet room tables sat eight each, and all but one of the conference attendees at her table seemed nice and eager to be here. The other woman appeared to think she was God's gift to songwriting and had her nose crammed so far up her rear end it was a wonder she bothered attending the conference. She seemed the type more liable to show up on an artist's doorstep demanding they use her music.

Then, of course, there were the important people. The twelve final-round judges were scattered amid the financial backers and industry bigwigs at the tables in the front of the room. She couldn't recall meeting any of the judges in person, but Taryn felt as though she'd met the man sitting next to Donald Shewson, the conference chair. The judge's sandy brown hair was closely cropped, and he wore wire-rimmed glasses that managed to make his already chiseled profile seem that much stronger.

"Cheesecake?"

Taryn looked to the woman standing next to her dressed in a tuxedo uniform and holding a delectable-looking piece of double-chocolate cheesecake. She smiled. "Like I could say no."

Dawn, the middle-aged blonde Taryn had been discussing workshops and the showcase performance with, laughed beside her. "Tell me about it." She patted a gently rounded stomach. "Only on you it doesn't show."

"Trust me, it does." *All in the hips and ass.*

"Ladies and gents." Donald Shewson's microphone -amplified voice rang out from the raised stage at the front of the room.

Taryn directed her attention toward Donald, only to have it landing on the head table Brian occupied instead. As if he felt her eyeing him, his head turned, and his gaze connected with hers. A slow, intimate smile curved his lips.

Her pulse accelerating, she forced herself to smile back before moving her focus on to Donald and the welcoming speech he gave from behind a podium. Only, it wasn't Donald's face filling her mind, but Brian's and his too-sexy smile.

"Why does his smile have to look so damned good?"

"I don't know that I'd call it good exactly, unless you're into sixty-year-olds, but as high up in the industry as he is, he seems pretty laid-back."

Taryn glanced at Dawn, frowning over the blonde's words. "Huh?"

"Donald." Dawn nodded toward the stage. "He seems nice, personable. Like maybe if I get stuck with him for the one-on-one icebreaker session, I might not lose my dinner over my nervousness."

"Right. Donald."

"Who were you talking about?"

"I was just…thinking about someone at home."

"I get it," Dawn said, but didn't look like she got it at all.

It was better that she didn't. Better that no one knew there was a past between her and Brian. Taryn planned to leave Sugar Foot with a number of important connections made, hoped to leave with the contract Saturday's showcase winners would receive. Brian played such a small part in the conference, their history shouldn't be an issue. Still, if the few should-have-been forgettable moments they'd shared jeopardized her plans, there would be some real hell to pay.

"Too bad too," a male voice put in from behind her.

Taryn tuned back into the conversation around her with the words. They were spoken by the man sitting next to Dawn. In his midthirties, he had a slow, Southern drawl, and before dinner, had worn a white cowboy hat.

"What's too bad?" she asked, wondering over what she'd missed while zoning out over unwanted thoughts of Brian.

Cowboy smiled at her, revealing a gap-toothed smile. "That we can't have relations with the conference staff. Couple of those ladies I was hoping to make a good impression with before the end of the week."

Taryn's belly tightened. "Relations with the staff?"

"I'd guess they mean physical," another man at the table offered.

"Physical?" Panic sliced through Taryn. *Which staff were they talking about?*

Dawn slammed her knee against Taryn's and, when Taryn looked over, mouthed, "Sex."

Taryn struggled to keep her voice calm. "What exactly do they mean by staff?"

With a quiet laugh, Cowboy nodded toward the stage. "Judges. Donnie there said if we get involved with any of them, we get booted from the conference."

Taryn breathed a sigh of relief. For a minute there, she thought she was in deep trouble. As she'd told Sarah, she didn't need this conference to make it in the songwriting industry, but that end of the week contract would still be a blessing.

"Yep. This thing's gonna be about pure talent," Cowboy said. "Not that I'm worried."

"You should be," Nose-Up-Her-Rear-End Lady said.

Cowboy's smile grew lopsided as he turned it on the brunette. He winked. "Just watch and see, honey. Before this week's out, you'll be agreeing I've got about the best chance of winning this thing out of everybody."

Nose-Up-Her-Rear-End Lady huffed, and Taryn exchanged an amused smile with Dawn.

"Before I wrap this up and get the week started," Donald continued, "I want you all to think about something, and that's heart, people. That's what making it in this business is all about. If you don't have the heart to invest in your music, you might as well not even try. Good luck this week and good night."

Taryn's smile fell away when she heard how closely Donald's words mimicked Brian's. Brian had used the word passion, but that was only a step away from heart.

"Thanks, Donald." Annie Joseph, a redhead who looked far too young to be a talent representative with Finish Line Records, took over the spot behind the podium. She turned to address the group. "As soon as everyone wraps up with that awesome dessert, we'll separate off into groups for the one-on-one icebreaker session by last names. A through D will meet with Mrs. Doran, E through H with Mr. Shewson, I through L with Mr. Macovney, M through P with Mr. Heald, Q through T with Ms. Stephens, and the lucky group in U through Z gets to meet with yours truly."

A collective laugh sounded through the banquet hall. Taryn joined in, but only until Brian's last name caught up with her. Why was he taking part in the icebreaker session? More importantly, what was her name doing falling in the group of people he would be meeting with?

Her attention zipped to his table, and, once again, his gaze locked with hers. Only this time, he didn't just flash an intimate smile. He grinned like a shark who'd spotted himself a nice, juicy tuna to devour.

Warpedly, her body responded to that grin, to the memory of the last time he'd looked upon her like he was about to consume her whole. Out on her balcony, right before he'd gone down on his knees and inhaled the aroused scent of her sex, which just so happened to be growing hot and moist even now. Something told her this icebreaker session with Brian would be anything but cold...and that, despite her vow to the contrary, before this week was through they would discover passion between them that extended well beyond lyrics.

Chapter Eight

"I didn't realize you would be taking part in any of the conference activities," Taryn said, after closing the door to a small, private interview room.

Brian gave her a reassuring smile as she took a seat on the chair across from him. He wasn't supposed to be handling the icebreakers, but one of the other judges was down with a stomach bug, and Donald Shewson asked him to take the guy's place tonight as a personal favor. That Taryn ended up in his group was pure fate. He was glad for it, though, as he hadn't had the chance to talk to her today, and he wanted to see if she was feeling okay.

While her skin didn't look nearly so red as last night, and her voice had been even, the anxiety in her tight-lipped expression and stiff posture told him that feeling okay would be the last way to describe her current state of mind. Apparently, she'd caught that part about contestants not having relations with the judges.

"One of the judges came down with a stomach bug. I'm filling in tonight only as a favor to Donald Shewson."

"Oh." Taryn smiled in a way that was clearly forced. The smile faltered, and she fidgeted in her seat, blurting, "We need to talk."

He could think of several ways to help ease those nerves. Unfortunately, all of them involved Taryn out of her far-too-modest black capris and white and black top. "Then you're in luck. Talking is what this session is intended for."

She stopped with her fidgeting to send him an irritated look. "You know what I mean, Brian. Not about the conference. About us."

"There's an us?"

"Yes. No." Her black eyebrows danced together, and the sunburned shade of her cheeks grew pinker. "That's not what I meant."

As tempting as it was to ask what she did mean, he had to focus on business. Though he already knew the questions from asking them to a number of others, Brian lifted the list from the small table next to his chair and pretended to study it. "Why don't you think about what you meant while I get started with the questions?"

"You idiot, this is important!"

He snapped his attention back to Taryn's face. She was glaring at him, her expression pure annoyance. It reminded him of the aggressive woman she was and made him ache to combat that aggressiveness with his own. That would mean getting up from this chair and crossing the short distance to hers, leaning over her, using his size to put her in place, make her feel like she didn't have to be so commanding all the time.

It would mean putting his hands on her body, tugging the simple shirt from the sensible capris and seeing what kind of lacy contraption she wore beneath. It would mean consuming those sassy, slightly too wide red lips until the only thing coming out of them would be moans.

It would mean that his mind was not on this conference.

Acknowledging the quickly hardening state of his dick, Brian bit back a groan. Business, damn it. He had to concentrate on business.

He set the list of questions aside and nodded. "You're right, Taryn, it is important. The impression you make on me now could very well influence the way I talk about you to the rest of the judges. Not that I need to tell you, I'm sure, but a big part of making it in this business, outside of being good at songwriting, is word of mouth and seeing that your name's traveling in the right circles. Give me something good to say about you." A surplus of good things filtered through his thoughts, all of them too personal and intimate to share, and he amended, "Something good you don't care if I share with others."

Slowly Taryn's annoyance faded, and she said, "Fine. Ask the questions."

"What's your biggest hope as a songwriter?"

Her mouth hitched up into an amused smile, and she laughed. "Could that question be any cheesier?" Brian started to suggest she respond, not commentate, when she continued, "Sadly, my answer's probably even more so. I've always dreamed of lying in my bed at night, too restless to fall asleep, so I turn on the radio and hear my song."

She sobered to add in a voice just above a whisper, "I wanted it to be your mom singing it, but I guess that won't be happening."

A knot of emotion came out of nowhere to lodge in Brian's throat while his gut tightened. He cleared his throat. "No, I guess not."

Why the reaction? People talked to him about his mother all the time; several of the interviewees had mentioned her tonight. It hadn't bothered him to discuss her with those others. With Taryn, she only had to say the words and he felt the hurt of losing his mother as acutely as if it had been yesterday. It had to be the note of reverence in Taryn's voice, the look of it in her eyes, the same one that had filled them the night she'd met Jacqueline. It was as if she'd cared about his mother not just as an idol, but as a person. It was as if she understood the intensity of his loss.

Brian chuckled, needing to move the conversation and the irrational thoughts along. She couldn't understand his loss, because she didn't even know how Jacqueline had died. "Trust me, Taryn, that's not so cheesy."

Her smile returned, and she closed her eyes. "That's not the cheesy part. The cheesy part is that I'm naked, stripped down to my truest self. Is that Freud for you or what?"

Freud or not, he couldn't say. The comment was, however, both the best way to move past thoughts of his mother's last painful days, and the worst way to keep this session strictly about the conference.

The vision of Taryn lying on her hotel bed, naked and helpless to resist his touch, the way she'd been last night, filled his mind and solidified his erection. She'd been out of control in those final moments before she'd come. Out of control and putty in his hands so pliant and delicious, he'd wanted to play with her all night long. Instead, he'd gone to the preconference meeting where he'd spent the night sipping on a single drink and acting like he was happy to be there. He hadn't been happy, or wanting to be there. He'd wanted to be back in Taryn's room, showing her that as good as that ice cream she'd moaned over might taste, it would be even better when licking it off each other.

Brian hadn't gotten to go back to her room and have ice cream or anything else, but that didn't mean he couldn't have something now. At least mentally. "Are you alone in bed?"

Taryn's eyes snapped open. "What?"

"I'm trying to get a visual. You know, for the purpose of understanding what your hopes are. It's important for me to fully grasp it...for the conference. So I can be sure to give my best impression of you to everyone else. Work with me. Are you alone, or with someone?"

Judging by the tension that had overtaken her body, Brian expected her to call him on the question, tell him just how inappropriate it was. Instead, she looked behind her at the window-slatted door, then back at him and smiled. This smile wasn't the forced one she'd first given him, or the dreamy one she'd had moments ago. This smile was the naughty, inviting one she'd worn when she'd opened her door to him in that sinfully seductive red dress.

Taryn closed her eyes again, relaxed in the chair. "I'm with someone," she said, her voice low, breathy. A total contrast to her proper business attire. "A man. He's naked too. And aroused. Hard. Throbbing."

Yes, he was. And Brian knew he should care about it, and the fact that they'd gotten completely off course. Only he couldn't care right now. He could only grin over the way she fell into the game.

She'd said that she loved a challenge, and he could guess her behavior had something to do with it. Either that, or she was setting him up for a serious fall and any second now planned to run to the door, toss it open, and accuse him of sexually harassing her to everyone standing nearby.

Hell, he was willing to chance it. "What's this man look like?"

"Mmm..." She shifted on her seat, rubbing her thighs together as if a hungry ache was building between them. "Tall. Sexy. Green eyes. I have a thing for green eyes. Dark features. A little beard stubble..."

Right on her neck, below the ear. She loved that. Shivered over it. Brian shivered now, remembering. "Is he touching you?" he asked roughly.

"Definitely." Taryn brought a hand up, caressed her fingers along the bare skin of her inner arm. "He's running his fingers up my arm. So softly, I can barely feel them and yet"—her breath wheezed out in a way that shot straight to his balls—"it's erotic somehow. It makes my nipples hard. My heart pound."

"Then what?" Brian sank down in his chair, needing to take the pressure off his cock. "Does he touch you anywhere else?"

"He sees how swollen my nipples are and has to touch them." She stroked her fingers up her arm and then down to her breast. He couldn't see the points of her nipples through her clothes, but he could guess they were erect. "He runs his fingers over them, and my breath catches." She strummed a thumb across her breast and gasped. "He grins at me, gives me that look that says he can see inside me, he knows what I want. How horny he's making me."

"Are you horny, Taryn?"

Her eyes snapped open. "What?"

"In this hope of yours. Remember, your biggest hope?"

"Right. My hope." She closed her eyes again, and the slow, seductive smile returned. "When he touches me that way, it drives me nuts. I want him *now*. But he won't let me have him now. He wants to take it slow. I let him because I know if I don't, he'll leave me on the edge. Just walk out of the room and won't come back."

Some of Brian's desire faded with the assessment.

Is that what she really thought of him, that he wanted to leave her the moment he got off? Maybe five years ago that had been true because he'd been embarrassed as hell and in need of an excuse to get away, but not two nights ago. She was the one who'd kicked him out then. And last night...he'd told her that he had no choice. "He doesn't sound very nice."

"I'm not sure yet. Maybe he is. Maybe not."

Did that mean she planned to get close enough again to decide? The ache of his groin intensified, and he was tempted to rub his dick through his pants. The way Taryn was sitting, she could risk touching herself without anyone besides him seeing her. Brian sat with his front half in plain view of the door's slatted windows, and given who was outside those doors, knew better than to tempt fate.

He bridged his fingers over his abdomen and asked in a rough voice, "So he was sucking on your nipples, then what?" Those hadn't been her exact words, but improvising had its place.

"Then he wants more. He moves down, licks all the way to my belly button." She ceased the stroking of her breast to slide her hand down her belly, lingering over the place where her navel would be. "He must have a belly button fascination, because he puts his tongue in it, runs it all around, thrusts it in and out, in and out." Her breath caught, and she licked her lips. "He's making me so hot. I want to come, but he's not moving fast enough."

Maybe not, but Brian had never wanted to move faster. He wanted to grab her out of that chair, lean her against the wall, pull down her pants, and thrust home. "But then he sees how close you are and goes faster."

"Yeah, he does." Taryn's hand continued its descent. She uncrossed her legs, parted them a few inches, and moved her fingers between. "He moves lower, uses his hands to pry my thighs apart. Not that he really needs to pry. I want to open for him. I want him inside me. But I don't get him. I just get his tongue."

Her fingers stroked between her thighs, rubbing against her crotch through her slacks. Her rapid breathing was a match to Brian's own. His nostrils flared, seeking out her musky scent. His tongue moved in his mouth, wanting to be where she'd placed it in her mind. "So wet," he murmured. "Slick. Hot."

"And it feels so good." The stroke of Taryn's fingers moved faster, pressed harder. "So good..."

"Then it gets even better," he added. "He stops licking and pushes his tongue inside your pussy. You can feel him, so far in, so deep. You can't hold on any longer. The sounds he's making, telling you how much he loves your sexy taste is too much. You can feel how aroused it's making him too. Feel him throbbing against your thigh."

She caught her lower lip in her teeth and joined her second hand with her first, strumming over her open body, caressing the growing need. She was close. Signs of it were everywhere, the sudden disjointed wheezes, the deepened pink of her cheeks. The way she squirmed on her chair.

He was close too. Close to forgetting where they were and what was at risk and taking her on that chair. Brian couldn't do that. He might not need to make a good impression at this conference, but Taryn did. For her, he fisted his hands and remained in his chair and let reckless hunger reflect in his words, "So you let it go. You feel that intense stabbing pressure, that magical tongue thrusting, thrusting, and you just. Can't. Hold. It. In."

"No. Can't. Do it." Her hands moved rapidly, rubbing, stroking, pressing furiously against her crotch through her capris as if she wanted to rip the pants off and bury her fingers knuckles-deep in her pussy. And then they stilled while her release came out on a strangled cry.

Several seconds passed before Taryn opened her eyes. She blinked. Then blinked again. A sheepish look claimed her face as she straightened in her seat. "Um, yeah. So that's my hope."

A soft knock sounded, and Brian looked past her to the woman at the door. He grunted. Why the hell did it always seem that right when he had Taryn where he wanted her, one of them had to leave?

He grinned then. Maybe she had to leave, but he'd have her back with him soon enough. She had to come back to him. If not because she couldn't resist the chemistry between them, then because she needed one more time with him to decide if he was a nice guy. "That's quite a hope, Taryn. I wish you the best of luck in seeing it come true. Now, I hate to rush you out of here, but they're signaling our time's up."

Taryn jerked her head around and noted the woman at the door. She turned back and stood, the color in her cheeks more vivid than ever. "Um, have a good night."

"I hope to. As soon as the interviews are over, I plan to go back to my room and see what I can find for entertainment. How about you?"

"I'll probably do that too."

"Go back to my room and see what you can find for entertainment?" he said teasingly. "Sounds like a dynamite plan to me."

Taryn's gaze flickered back to his, and heat charged in her eyes. "Yes. No. Time's up," she finally decided on and hurried out the door.

Chapter Nine

Holding the hotel room phone to her ear, Taryn kicked off her shoes and flopped back on the bed. When the ringing on the other end was cut off with a too-cheerful hello, she groaned. She really ought to look into getting a new best friend, one who didn't sound so damned carefree. At least not when Taryn felt like her life was being mixed up in a blender set on psycho speed.

"I'm so confused." She moaned into the receiver.

The enthusiasm left Sarah's voice as she said drily, "Hello to you too."

"Yeah, hello. Sorry. I'm just..." Turning into a huge flake. "He is driving me bonkers, Sarah!"

"'He' meaning Brian?"

"Yes!"

After the way she'd caved to his totally inappropriate challenge and then hightailed it out of that interview room like a coward, Taryn no longer had a clue what her next move would be with Brian. "One second I'm convinced I can't stand him and need to avoid him at all costs, and the next second he's talking me into getting myself off when all we're supposed to be doing is breaking the ice."

Sarah laughed. "I don't know, honey, sounds like he had you melting it to me."

"That's exactly the problem. I shouldn't even be talking to him."

"You said that before you left, though. If things have changed—"

"I don't mean I don't *want* to talk to him—I don't know if I do or not. I mean that he served as a stand-in judge today, and talking with the judges about anything other than the conference is hugely taboo. Knowing what one of them looks like without their clothes on is a good way to get my butt kicked off this place." Taryn had gone into the icebreaker session prepared to cement his agreement that he wouldn't say a word about their physical involvement and to make it clear that involvement was over, regardless that he wasn't a true judge. But then he'd thrown that damned challenge at her, and she couldn't tell him no, despite how harmful giving in could be.

Hell, she hadn't even considered telling him no for more than a few seconds. He'd tossed out the bait, and she followed it in all the way to his rod.

"Does he still look as good naked?"

Taryn's racing thoughts came to a standstill. "Are you serious? I told you there's a potential of my getting booted out of this conference, which you know could mean my songwriting career's life or death, and all you heard is that I know what he looks like without his clothes on?"

Sarah let out an exaggerated sigh. "Of course, I heard the rest—I have this habit of listening to you even when you're acting like a total spaz—but since you told me less than a month ago that you don't need this conference to make it, I chose to look past the rest. Really, Taryn, I don't see what you're so confused about. So he talked you into getting yourself off. He still hasn't been able to accomplish that task himself, right?"

Taryn climbed off the bed to pace. She needed to occupy at least part of her body so her mind wouldn't be tempted to recall the way Brian had made her come undone. It didn't work. The memory of his big fingers rocking up inside her repeated in her mind and liquefied her pussy.

She stopped in front of the mirrored closest door, stuck out her tongue, and made a face. *Mmm...attractive.*

Maybe if she looked like that the next time she was around Brian, it would convince him to keep his distance, and she'd be able to keep hers in return.

"Taryn? Has Brian made you come?"

Taryn's reflection frowned at her. She didn't want to respond, because Sarah would undoubtedly find some way to confuse her all the more once she knew the answer. "He was using his hands not his body. And I was probably really easy because I was so tired, not to mention twice-baked. I don't even know how he could find me appealing, I was so freaking red at the time."

"You know, I hear that not all men are so shallow, they only want a woman for what she looks like. Maybe he's one of those guys."

Yep, just as predicted, Sarah was trying to confuse her all the more by making Brian sound appealing. Obviously her friend had forgotten his less than finer points. "This is Brian we're talking about, Sarah. Brian Macovney. The ego-ruled corporate raider. The guy that eats little people for breakfast. The guy who couldn't go the distance in bed if he had to. Remember him?"

"I do, but what about you?"

"What do you mean?"

"If you're so sure the guy you just described is the Brian there now, why are you even bothering to call me and talk about him? Why be confused at all? If he's such an ass, why not forget about him and move on to someone else?"

Because she couldn't, damn it!

Taryn had tried to move on to someone else, but each time Brian magically appeared and made her body decide it wanted to give him another chance. Most of it was her body. Only one small part was her mind's doing; the part that kept reminding her that while today he'd seemed more concerned about playing than learning about her, yesterday he'd appeared genuinely interested in her songwriting.

She paced back to the bed and sank down on the side before answering. "He said he'd help with my music."

"Help do what with it?"

"It lacks passion."

"That just occurred to you?" Sarah asked, sounding skeptical.

"Brian pointed it out." Taryn rushed on before Sarah could comment, "But he's right. I can see that now. He offered to help me put the passion into it. When I asked why he would help, he said because he likes to help people. He said everything I've ever heard or read about him is fabricated."

"You believe it?"

"Of course not!"

Okay, so maybe some part of her wanted to, the same part that kept thinking about the way he'd behaved after hearing her music. The very same part that couldn't help but recall the honest affection he'd harbored for his mother. Taryn had only seen the two interact once, but it had been enough to make her believe Brian completely supported his mother's career.

And now he seemed to want to support Taryn's.

Unless appearance was all there was to it. He came off as wanting to help, but really had no such intention to do so. The evidence against him was rather damning. "This is the same guy who called me an aggressive, sexual control freak two nights ago. That is not something a nice guy does."

"So you aren't going to accept his offer of help?"

"No." Only what if there was more to his offer than appearance? What if he'd been sincere? She could hardly afford to be wrong about that. Not with the showcase five days away and a performance song that was decent at best. Hell. "Okay, so yes, I am. At least, maybe. I don't know." Taryn sank back on the bed and sighed. "I'm so confused."

"Well, if nothing else, you have that much figured out," Sarah said drily, then sobered to add, "How about you confront Brian? Ask him if he's such a nice guy to prove it. Then ask him if he can go the distance in bed to prove that to you too."

Taryn bolted to a sitting position. She held the phone to her ear in a death grip. She was either hearing Sarah wrong, or her friend had fallen off the proverbial rocker. "You're suggesting I sleep with him again?"

"It's just an idea."

Yeah, Sarah had fallen off the rocker to make that really, really bad suggestion. The really, really bad suggestion that sounded way too damned tempting considering Taryn knew how awful things would turn out.

"Okay, I'll think about it." She would think about it, just as she'd been doing since arriving at Sugar Foot, but that was as far she would take it. She might continue to contemplate his offer of help with her songwriting, might even decide to take him up on it, but there was no way she would be getting horizontal with him again—to prove what kind of guy he was, or for any other reason.

And on that note, time to get away from the subject of Brian altogether. "So, how are things going with work? Is Laurel stalking you?"

Sarah sighed dramatically, and Taryn could visualize her rolling her eyes. "Let's just say she stops by every day and flies around my desk like a bat on steroids. Other than that, everything's great."

"Good, because if I thought things were too hectic for—"

"You're not coming home until the week's over, so don't even finish that sentence," Sarah reprimanded, then before Taryn could comment, followed it up with, "So, you never told me."

"Told you what?"

"If he still look as good with his clothes off."

Ugh. Back to Brian. Worse, back to thoughts of Brian naked.

Unwittingly, Taryn allowed the image of him on the beach yesterday afternoon to fill her mind. She'd barely gotten her response out to his question of if she was asking him to strip, when he was naked and semierect, and she was gawking like a schoolgirl. If she hadn't been turned on by the idea of standing in front of him naked on an occupied beach, then she'd grown so in that instant. A lot like she was doing now, remembering the way his long, lean body had moved as he'd played volleyball. His tan lines were in just the right places to really call out certain attributes.

Taryn sighed. "Does the thought of Johnny Depp in the buff make you drool?"

Sarah laughed. "I'll take that as a yes. And repeat what I said before—confront him, Taryn. Though it seems the sun down there has baked your brain enough to make you forget you are a strong woman, one of the ballsiest I know. Don't be afraid of him, hon. Live up to that aggressive title he's given you and let him hear you roar. Now I gotta go. Company just arrived."

"Company? At...it's almost midnight there. On a Tuesday night."

"Yep." Sarah sounded delighted. "You aren't the only one melting ice this week. I might keep lucky guy number six around a while too."

"Seriously?" Sarah settling down with a lone man, at least for more than a week; now there was something Taryn never saw coming.

Sarah's bark of laughter cut through the phone line. "No," she finally said. "But I thought I'd give you something else to think about for a few seconds. Bye, hon. And remember, let him hear your roar."

Chapter Ten

The loud knocking on Brian's hotel room door was punctuated by a familiar and desperate-sounding "Hurry up!"

He went to the door and opened it a fraction; then it was pushed in the rest of the way. Taryn stood at the threshold, looking one way then the other so quickly, she reminded him of a bobblehead doll gone mad. "Tar—"

"Get out of the way," she said with a growl. With a last look around, she pushed him aside and hurried into the room. "Now close the door!"

He did as she asked, then turned around to find her standing in the middle of the room, her eyes wild, hair hanging half out of a ponytail holder, and breath coming out in ragged gasps. She'd either just finished having sex or was running from something or someone.

The thought of her sleeping with another man twisted Brian's guts, so he grabbed hold of the second idea. "What are you running from, or who?"

"Not running. Trying not to be spotted."

He went from concerned to stimulated as the reason for her behavior reached him. He'd indicated she should stop by for entertainment. Obviously, she'd decided to take him up on his offer and feared getting caught in the act.

Brian had been semiaroused since she'd walked out of the icebreaker session. Thoughts of the eager way she'd ground her clothed pussy against her fingers refused to be extinguished, and it was tempting to give in by crossing the room and pulling Taryn into his arms. It was even more tempting to make her admit what it was she'd come here for. Making her ask for what she wanted was the first step in getting her to see how good being submissive could feel.

Crossing his arms, he leaned back against the door and smiled knowingly. "So, are you lost, or was there something on your mind?"

"I need passion."

Well that had been a whole hell of a lot easier than he'd guessed it would be. He uncrossed his arms and took purposeful steps toward her, letting his gaze roam over her body as he went. She'd changed out of the sedate business attire into simple white cotton shorts and a matching tank top. A lot of pinkish tan skin stood out. A lot more would be out in just a few seconds. His cock throbbed with anticipation, and he heightened his strides.

Taryn's eyes went wide. She shook her head in another mad bobblehead move. "I meant I need— want—your help with getting the passion into my songs."

Feeling like he'd been doused with ice water, Brian stopped a few feet short of reaching her. His smile fell.

Her songs. Right.

Fuck, he should have known, even after what happened earlier, her coming to his room for sex would be too much to ask for when she learned about the "no relations with the conference staff" rule. But then, what she was here for was almost as unethical. "What happened to being worried about getting caught?"

Wariness flashed in her eyes, but she shrugged. "You said you're a nice guy. You also said you wouldn't get me in trouble."

He *was* a nice guy, one who was eager to help Taryn, particularly when she was giving him a chance to prove the negative press on him was little more than rumors. She'd probably miss that he was being nice, but in time she'd figure it out.

Brian took another step toward her. He again allowed his attention to drift down her curvy body to long, shapely legs he'd thought about being wrapped around his waist far too much these last days. His groin pulsed with the memories. He returned his gaze to her boobs, remembered the hot taste of them beneath his tongue, the urgent press of her nipples into his mouth that night on her balcony.

She hadn't given him time to savor. He would soon. Just not tonight. Tonight was solely for taunting.

Crowding her in with another step, he pierced her breasts with his hungry gaze. "So it's okay if we fuck?"

With a tiny gasp, Taryn shuffled backward toward the floor-to-ceiling entertainment center. She wrapped her arms tightly over her chest, as if she thought cloaking the luscious objects of his attention would be enough to stop his advances. "That won't be happening."

Brian moved another foot forward, into her personal space. Inches from touching her nipples with his fingertips. They were peaked now and pressing hard against her tank top. *Putty in my hands.* He couldn't help but feel a bit of conceit and a whole lot of testosterone.

"You want it to happen, Taryn." Lust deepened his voice, thundered through his veins. "You want me bad."

Her breathing sounded faster. She took another step back—the last step she could take before running into something—and swallowed visibly. Her attention darted around the room, side to side, floor to ceiling. Realizing she was caged brought her gaze slamming back to his. The blue of her irises went dark as midnight, and a second, louder gasp escaped her throat.

"Only in your ego-ruled mind," she squeaked out.

"No way, babe. You want me, and I can prove it."

A response rounded her lips. Before she could get it out, he advanced on her. Taking the final step back had her ass hitting the entertainment center, and her eyes flaring wide.

He grinned mercilessly. *Gotcha.*

Primal male instinct slammed through him, solidifying his dick. Taking her wrists in his hands, he dragged her arms over her head, up against the hard wood so that her breasts were thrust tauntingly forward. The blood pounded between his ears and then jetted swiftly to his balls. The brush of his lips over hers was intense in its gentleness, intended as the perfect surprise to her expectations. He pulled away, and she whimpered low, hungrily, near silently demanding more.

Goal one met.

"Tell me you don't want this." With the grind of his aching cock against her belly, he returned his lips to hers.

This kiss was no bare caress, but an all-out mouth-fuck that should have rocked every one of her senses. Taryn's mouth was still against his impaling, her tongue unresponsive. The increased pressure of his dick against her belly met with the same lack of response, and that just plain pissed him off.

Capturing both of her wrists in one hand, Brian pushed his other hand under her tank top, past the lace of her bra. Her nipple was rock solid, hot beneath his touch. He squeezed the bud between finger and thumb, and the moan that fed from her lips to his was the greatest balm for his ego. She was bothered by him, all right. Hot and horny and bothered to the point she would soon be demanding control. And he would soon be fucking her up against this entertainment center if he didn't get his point across and finish this interlude damned fast.

As if on cue, Taryn attempted to take control. She quit the immobile game, and her tongue went to work against his, licking, sucking, devouring. Her body molded decadently against his. Trapping his hand between their chests, she rose on tiptoe to answer the grinding of his sex with the mad circling of her own. Then she quit with the circling to draw her hips back and thrust against his dick.

A growl erupted from his throat. Goal two met, and mission past the point of accomplishment if he didn't quit this shit and remember his intention immediately.

Holding tightly to her wrists, he broke from her lips and put distance between them. "Tell me you don't want me. That it doesn't drive you crazy when I take control." Her eyes narrowed, and he laughed. "You love feeling helpless, Taryn. It makes your pussy sop with wetness."

"I'm not wet."

He closed the slight gap between them and shoved his hand down the front of her shorts. Cupped the sweet curve of her crotch. Juices soaked through her panties and leaked onto his palm. Too fucking sexy. "Try again."

"It's not from you. I indulged myself with a finger fuck before I came over."

He let go a rough chuckle. "Keep talking that way, and I promise I'll turn you around, pull down these shorts, and push into this snug little pussy from behind."

Her breathing grew faster. Her hips pistoned, pressing her cunt hard against his palm. Belying the visceral move, she bit out, "I don't want that!"

"Okay." He pulled his hand from her shorts.

Confusion and disappointment warred over her features. "Okay?"

The look was priceless. Freeing her wrists was bound to throw her even more off-kilter. Only goal three was still underway.

Keeping his hold on her wrists, Brian brought his free hand to her face and caressed the rise of a sunburned cheek. "Okay...if you'd rather I did you slow. What do you say I drag you over to the bed, strip you naked, and tie you sunny-side up. I'll start with my hands, along your legs, over your thighs, across your ass. You'll love being spanked. A few swats. Then a few more, harder. I'll keep it going till your butt's on fire because the pain hurts so good. Then I'll move to your pussy, give it a little pummeling from behind. And you'll keep loving it. You'll be so wild, you'll burn for me. And then, Taryn—then I'll do it some more. Just keep going, slow and steady, easy but firm, spanking you, fingering you, fucking you with my tongue until you beg me to come."

Her nostrils flared. Chest heaved with the force of her breathing. Hesitation and excitement mingled in her eyes. "You can't make me do anything. You suck at sex."

Brian brought his face close to hers, forcing her to look into his eyes, to see the intensity of them. "I don't suck, and you know it. The two climaxes I gave you, or at least helped give you, in as many days tell you that. They tell you that I'm exactly what I claim to be—a man who knows how to please a woman. They also tell you what you are—an aggressive, sexual control freak."

Taryn stiffened on a hiss. He pulled back enough she could see his smile. "I'm such a nice guy, I'm willing to help you fix your little problem. I'm willing to help you see it's okay to be the submissive one. It's okay to give in to your fears."

"I'm not afraid," she retorted, but her voice trembled.

His gut roiled with the sound. He hadn't believed she would be truly afraid, no matter what he did. Now, he knew differently.

She was still highly aroused, but also showing fear. Fear that wasn't directed at him, Brian realized, and still fear that made him want to forget about this whole charade. To release her and be the shoulder she clearly needed.

Only he knew better than to think Taryn would readily accept a shoulder, least of all his. She was like so many of the dominant types he dealt with through business. They didn't want to be coddled. They wanted to be helped in a way that the end result seemed all their own doing. That self-seeking desire is how he managed to keep the truth about his business dealings quiet. No one was about to admit what he'd done for them when it would mean losing the face of the triumphant leader themselves.

If he was going to help Taryn, then he had to finish this the way he'd started. With the intent of riling her, pissing her off to the point of fury.

"I think you are afraid, maybe not of sex, but something. Something that affects even this. Even us." Quickly, he shoved his hand back into her shorts, this time past her panties as well. Her bare mound insistently pressed to his palm. He answered that press, parting her slit and sinking a finger up inside her pussy.

A rush of hot air escaped Taryn's mouth. She tried and failed to still her hips. "There is no us! I don't even like you!"

"Are you sure?" The desperate clenching of her sex around his finger said otherwise. "It feels like you like me. It feels like you like me a whole lot."

Brian added a second finger, worked them together inside her slick walls. Withdrawing them slightly had her instinctively following, bringing her a few inches away from the entertainment center and then a few more when he repeated the move once and again. He moved faster that last time, enough to unsettle her. He released her wrists, and she checked her step and then clung to his forearm for balance. He turned his newly free hand on her ass, yanked down her shorts and panties, and gave her bare backside a loud, resounding *crack* that echoed through the hotel room and rushed a wheeze from her mouth.

Taryn's eyes darted to his face, a mixture of shock and loathing. He swatted her butt a second time and felt the pleasing response in the sudden deluge of her pussy. Knew that same response as the pained tugging of his balls.

"Like that, don't you? Told you that you would. If you want me to keep going, all you have to do is ask. Or are you afraid to say the words for fear of what will come out of your mouth?"

She shook her head violently, knocking the ponytail holder free and sending shoulder-length black hair cascading around her face. She looked wild, sexy, and confused as hell. "Yes," she finally said, followed by a resigned, "No." Then, "I don't know. You make me nuts, you asshole!"

Goal three met. Mission accomplished.

Smirking, he pulled his fingers from her sex. Pried her hands off his forearm. Righted her on her feet and settled her clothing back into place. "Then my plan's working perfectly."

She started in on the head shaking again. Reconciled to the fact she wasn't going to leave unless he moved her out of the room himself, Brian took hold of her and moved her to the door. He opened the door and set her outside.

Taryn found her voice on an incredulous, "What are you doing?"

"Being a bastard and kicking you out. That's what I do, right? Get you hot and bothered, then walk away. Just living up to your expectations."

He shut the door until only a fraction of her stunned face was visible. "Here's a thought, instead of standing there with your mouth hanging open and risking your spot in this conference, why not go back to your room and get out how you feel, how much you can't stand me right now. How much you hate me, or maybe how much you don't hate me. Whatever wild thoughts are spinning around in your head, write them down. Then when you're done, come back here and we'll see if we can't make some music out of it."

Taryn's gasp sounded along with the closing of the door.

Chapter Eleven

Not a nice guy. Nope. Nuh-uh. Brian was *so* not a nice guy.

But he did know how to get her creative juices, among others, flowing.

Taryn had gone over to his room ready to lay down the rules and roar. She hadn't managed to do either, but she was managing to write up a storm.

Passion had to be rioting through her body and directly into her fingertips, because she'd been writing lyrics since she'd returned to her room over an hour ago, and they were good. They felt good anyway. Too good to be bad.

But what if she was fooling herself? What if these lines were just as lacking as all the others she'd written through the years?

Hell, she didn't want to have self-doubt. For one thing she didn't have anything to drown the insecurity with—namely a pint or six of good-quality ice cream—and for another, she wouldn't fall asleep so long as it lingered at the fringes of her mind.

What she needed was a critique by someone who knew what they were talking about. Someone like…oh…Brian.

Going to him after the way he'd treated her would make her look desperate. Not to mention flighty. But he had said to come back when she was ready to share. And making a move that could help further her career wasn't really desperate, but logical.

O-kay. So good. She was being logical. Her father would be proud.

Taryn snorted. The day her father was proud of anything related to her songwriting would be a cold one. Her father and others like him, both those who believed songwriting a hobby more than a career and those who said she didn't have what it took to make it regardless, were the reasons she needed to take her lyrics to Brian. Songwriting would never be just a hobby to her, and she did have what it took. She would succeed, even if it meant kowtowing to the last man she wanted to kowtow to.

Before she could change her mind, Taryn grabbed the sheets of hotel stationery she'd scribbled the music on. Lines had been flowing from the moment Brian shut his door in her face, and she hadn't wanted to take the time to dig through her stuff for either better paper or her laptop. She pushed her feet into flip-flops and started for the door. The blackness that drifted in through the open windows, along with the balmy evening breeze, had her coming to a halt and glancing at the bedside alarm clock.

It was late. After one in the morning. Dare she go over there now? Odds were good he was asleep. Odds were better that if he wasn't asleep and she came knocking on his door this time of night, he'd assume she was there to discuss passion of an altogether other kind. He'd have no qualms about shoving his fingers back into her panties, or swatting her ass a few more times. Her butt tingled with the thrill she'd gotten from the smack of his hand. No man had ever spanked her. No matter how shockingly wet it had gotten her, no man ever would spank her again. At least no man named Brian. They were just wrong together.

W-R-O-N-G.

And that still didn't solve her current dilemma.

Maybe she could call. But no, she couldn't call— even if he wasn't awake, the ringing of the phone would make him that way. She'd just have to wait until morning...and be a zombie all day because she hadn't managed to sleep a wink.

Clearly there was only one answer here. She had to risk sneaking back over to his room and trying to knock. Just once. Real softly. If he opened the door, which was unlikely, she'd worry about getting her reason for being there across.

Five minutes later, Taryn rounded the hallway that led to Brian's eighth-floor hotel room. She listened for voices and, noting no sign of life, dashed for his door. She knocked once, softly. Ten seconds passed with no answer. She tried again a bit longer, harder. Another twenty seconds passed. No answer. Damn it.

With a quick glance around to make sure the coast was still clear, she rapped long and hard, then threw in a, "Brian, open the damned door!" for good measure.

He opened the door after a few seconds, barefoot and wearing a rumpled T-shirt and shorts. From his heavy-lidded eyes to his tousled hair, he looked tired, so she smiled sweetly. "I didn't wake you, did I?"

"Pounding on my door and yelling my name, now how could that be?"

"Sorry. I just..." Just was standing where anyone could see her. She pushed past him into his room and noted his still-made bed. Despite his appearance, he hadn't been sleeping. Good. She wanted him clear minded when he read her lyrics.

Before he could get the idea she'd come here for another reason, Taryn spun around and thrust the papers in her hands at him. "Here."

Brian shut the door and yawned, before nodding at the papers. "What are those?"

Guilt edged up with that yawn. She should have waited until morning. Realizing he wasn't going to take the papers, she pulled her hands back. "My song. The one you made me write. It's not finished, but it's close. I was going to have you read it, but it can wait until morning."

She moved past him and reached for the door handle. His hand on her arm stopped her. "I didn't make you write anything, Taryn."

The heat of his hand on her bare arm felt hot enough to singe. She turned back and looked up at his face so close to hers. His beard stubble was dense, and the memory of the way it felt rubbing along her skin threatened to make her forget her purpose. "The one you inspired me to write then," she said quickly.

He nodded and released her arm. "Now you're getting it. Inspiration is what passion is all about. Particularly at this stage in your career, you should concentrate on writing about things that inspire you. Things you've been through or seen someone else go through. In order to move others, you first need to be moved yourself. " He held out a hand. "Let me see what you've got."

Taryn handed the papers to him and made her way across the room to the sitting area. She pulled a chair out from under the small table and sat on it cross-legged. Brian was either too tired or too focused on helping her to do so much as drop a sexual innuendo. Since she wasn't tired enough or focused enough to forget about either sexual innuendos or the main event itself, she was glad to be out of close range from him.

"When I'm reading, you can eat," he said as he went to the minifridge and squatted. He pulled a pint of Chocolate Cashew Heaven from the freezer, and her heart almost stopped.

How could she think he wasn't a nice guy when he kept lavishing her with her favorite ice cream? Aware her smile was bright enough to light up the entire island, she accepted the ice cream. "Where do you keep getting this from?"

He returned her smile with a grin as he lifted a plastic spoon off the counter and gave it to her. "If I told you, I wouldn't have a secret weapon, now would I? Just say thank you, woman. It isn't that hard."

And neither was looking at him when he was grinning like that. It was his sexy grin, the one that could do her in like no other. It was a damned good thing he was tired and that she was armed with

Chocolate Cashew Heaven, or bad things that felt way too incredibly good surely would be happening.

"Thank you." Taryn pulled the lid off the container and set it on the table. Her belly gave an excited rumble as she dipped the spoon into the rich chocolate, marshmallow and cashew-swirled ice cream. She lifted the spoon to her mouth, then feeling Brian's gaze on her, looked at him to ask, "Do you want a bite?"

He looked like he wanted to laugh, and she could only guess her expression had morphed into her "I'm about to eat this whole pint of ice cream, hallelujah" face. "Go ahead." He took a seat on the bed and turned his attention on her papers. "I'm okay for now."

"Yeah, well, you'd better be okay for now and later, because once I start eating, I'm not stopping until the carton's empty."

* * *

Could she moan any more if she tried?

Brian had taken great pleasure in watching Taryn eat the first few bites of ice cream. Actually devour would be a better way to describe how she tackled the pint. Her eyes shone while her mouth curved in an elated smile that managed to stay put even as she scooped ice cream into her mouth. Those first few bites, the sight of her happiness over something so trivial had warmed him in a place he'd let very few touch these last years. Then she caught him watching her for the second time, and he'd returned his attention to her lyrics.

And the moans had reached him.

Rationally he knew the sounds were aimed at the ice cream, and that she probably wasn't even aware she was making them. Irrationally he couldn't help but notice how much they sounded like the moans she made right before she climaxed. Brian had fallen asleep on the love seat while watching TV. Taryn's knocking and ensuing shouting had wakened him. He was still somewhat groggy, and that had to be the reason his body responded to the irrational thought.

Moving back against the bed's headboard, he placed a pillow over his lap to hide his quickly swelling cock. Then to stop her from wondering over the move, set all but one of the music sheets on it, as if he was using it for a makeshift table.

He forced all thoughts of her and every one of her ecstatic noises from his mind to concentrate on her music. He hadn't given her a fair interview this afternoon; the least he could do was read her lyrics and give some feedback.

He smiled over the title "You Drive Me Nuts." It was amusing, given it was one of the last things she'd said to him before he'd closed the door on her, and he was mildly surprised she hadn't included the "you asshole" part, as well.

Brian moved on to the first line, impressed by its potency, and by the third one found himself skipping words. By the fifth line, his heart was beating faster, and he realized how hard he was smiling. He forced his mouth to flatten out and his eyes to move slower to take in each word.

When he reached the final line on the last sheet of paper, his heart was thudding, and his smile threatened to return. He pushed it away again and set the papers aside. He felt Taryn's gaze on him. How long had she been watching him? Whether it was because the alternating annoyed and exultant words sounded like they were directed at him or the angst-ridden song really was that good, he'd become completely invested in it.

Just in case it was the former reason and others wouldn't find it so moving, he stuck with a safe response. "Mmm..."

Taryn's hand, laden with a heaping spoonful of ice cream, stilled halfway to her mouth while her gaze narrowed. "Mmm? What does 'mmm' mean? And don't you dare say that it's nice, or I swear I'll stick this spoon somewhere you'll need professional help getting it back out."

He chuckled. "I wasn't going to say it was nice."

"I don't want to hear good, either." She waved the spoon at him like if one bad word came out of his mouth, she would follow up on her threat.

"It isn't good."

The ice cream-induced sparkle left her eyes. She slapped the spoon on the table and gripped her belly. "I think I'm going to be sick. I thought it was good. It felt so good when I was writing it. I was sure—"

"It's better than good, Taryn." Brian knew he should have kept the truth to himself until she had the chance to get a second opinion, but he couldn't handle seeing her insecurities laid out there so plainly and painfully.

She lifted her hand from her stomach, and hope filled her eyes. "For real?"

Hell she was a hard woman to keep up with. One day it seemed his was the last opinion she wanted, and the next it seemed she was hinging her happiness on it. He should say something to rile her again, make her forget that she cared what he thought. Make her remember her dominant personality, which he was beginning to think more and more was at least a partial facade.

He didn't say anything to rile her, because he wanted her to understand he was being sincere. "I wouldn't lie to you about your music. *Now*, I wouldn't," he clarified. "Not when I know how important it is to you."

Something flickered through Taryn's eyes, some unnamable emotion, then she said, "Oh," and returned to eating.

Brian was tempted to ask about that emotion. He didn't because emotions were not supposed to be involved in their relationship. Him helping her reach her fullest potential, yes. Carnal gratification and teaching her a thing or two about submissive sex, definitely. But never feelings.

Needing to lighten the mood, he nodded at the papers on the pillow over his lap. "So if I was the inspiration for these lyrics, I guess you were pretty ticked off at me when you left earlier. Have you forgiven me?"

Taryn's lips curved into a smile that turned rapturous as she put another chocolate-and-marshmallow heaping spoonful into her mouth. She sighed heartily. "The ice cream helps."

So would keeping his brain above his waistline, Brian thought as his finally relaxed dick tightened anew. Sexual gratification could be a part of their relationship, but it would not be taking place tonight. He'd vowed to make this night about helping her, and he intended to keep that promise. "What if I said I thought your song was more than better than good? What if I thought, with just a bit of tweaking and some lengthening, it will be great, quite possibly enough so to win one of the contracts on Saturday."

She dipped the spoon into the carton, took a leisurely bite, and then placed both spoon and carton on the table. Her smile gone, she stood. "I'd say you were trying to get in my pants, and that I've stayed too long."

Taryn started for the door, and Brian said, "I think we'd both agree that earlier proved that if I wanted to get in your pants, I would be there."

She stopped and turned back, confusion clear on her face. And maybe, just maybe, disappointment. "You don't want to be in my pants?"

Oh, yeah, there was disappointment there. He grinned and patted the mattress next to his thigh. "You could always try to persuade me."

For several seconds, as her gaze swept the length of him then zeroed in on the pillow over his lap, he thought she would do just that. Then she looked away and shook her head. "I don't want you in my pants. I was just...never mind. It's late. I need to go."

It was late, but he wasn't tired any longer, and he still owed Taryn the chance to answer the icebreaker questions. He needed to know her answers for the sake of being able to critique her fairly and share his insight with the judges. Or so that's the reason he'd claim if she pressed him on the matter. That he wanted to know about her for the sake of his curiosity, he'd worry about later. "Are you tired?"

"A little, but I'm probably still too jazzed from writing to fall asleep. You're tired, though."

"Not so much anymore. Besides, I don't have to be anywhere until ten, so I can sleep late. Let's finish the icebreaker interviewer."

"Finish it how?"

Her skeptical look spoke her thoughts loud and clear. She believed he was back to thinking about sex. That he was lounging on the bed, his hand still reclining on the spot he'd patted, didn't help matters.

His body calm enough to remove the pillow without worrying her, Brian stood. He went to the small table and pulled out a chair across from the one she'd occupied. "For starters," he said, as he sat, "by you telling me how you became interested in songwriting in the first place."

Taryn returned to her chair. "It started out as a fanciful dream I had as a girl. I always loved your mom's music—so many of her songs seemed to be about me." She smiled, and the pink of her sunburned cheeks grew darker. "Probably eighty percent of the population thought they were about them at some point in time, but it still made me want to be like her. Bummer for me I couldn't sing—at least, not good enough to get anywhere—so I tried writing a song since it seemed almost as good as singing. I shared what I wrote with my friends, who all assured me it

was awful. Pure crap, I believe were the exact words,"
she said with a wince. "So I quit writing."

Ouch. That wince spoke of old hurt that she might
think she'd moved past, but obviously she hadn't.
"Knowing how determined you are, I can't believe you
would let girls who were probably jealous of your talent
influence you?"

Her smile fell, and she looked at him blankly. For
the second time since she entered his room, Brian had
to fight the urge to ask what was on her mind.

The blank look passed, and she said, "I was really
young then, hardly even a teenager. I started writing
again my senior year in high school and knew it was
better than singing could ever be. It was everything I'd
ever imagined it would be and more. I loved it." She
shrugged. "But songwriting's not exactly the kind of
thing you can just get a job in, so I went to college and
graduated with a degree in business."

What about the four or five years in between high
school and obtaining her degree? She was holding
something back. But, damn it, he didn't dare press for
an answer that was bound to have some hefty
emotional strings attached. "How did you get started
on the commercial jingles?"

Taryn's smile returned, and she laughed. "That
was a mistake. I was at work one day when this
announcer came on the radio and mentioned a slogan
contest for shoe deodorizer, of all things. I spouted off
some cheeseball lines just to amuse myself. Sarah
wrote them down without telling me and sent them
into the radio station, and—wham—two months later

the product owner was calling me to offer a contract. He loved my warped sense of humor."

What man wouldn't?

Brian shook the thought away to ask, "Sarah is…"

"My friend and colleague."

"Speaking of which, what about your business? You said you own a promotional company."

"Actually, I sort of improvised when I said that. Sarah and I co-own Lasting Impressions."

Improvised to impress him? No, at the time she had still hated him, so it had been improvising for the sake of making herself look good. How did she feel about him now? Was the jury still out, the way she'd said this afternoon? Damn, he shouldn't care how she felt. "You would walk away from your company and Sarah to pursue your songwriting career full-time?"

"The company in a heartbeat. I like doing promotional work—and, yeah, the occasional commercial jingle is great—but my heart isn't in those things. My heart's in songwriting, even if it doesn't always come through in my music. And Sarah's the one who convinced me to come here. She's my number one supporter. No matter what happens, we'll always be friends."

Then she did have someone at home who believed in her. For a while there, he hadn't been sure. "You want stardom?"

"I want to write, because I love it. I don't care about fame or fortune or…whatever. I want to do something I believe in, and know that others believe in me too."

"They will. I do."

As had happened before when Brian backed her talent, an unnamable emotion flickered through her eyes. Before she'd passed it off by changing the subject. This time Taryn looked like she wanted to talk about it.

Long seconds of silence passed as he waited for her to start. Finally, she said in a quiet voice, "What happened with your mom, Brian? It was like one day she was perfectly fine, and the next she was gone."

She sounded so sad about it. He, himself, felt nauseated. Tension sliced through him and his gut churned. "She was sick."

"I know, but how? It was so sudden. I still remember hearing about her death like it was yesterday. I was on my way to work when the newscast came on the radio. I wanted to turn around and go back to bed in the hopes it was a bad dream."

It *was* a bad dream. One that had lasted for months. Not that Taryn or anyone else but Brian would know that. His father knew how long his mother had been sick, of course, but he'd been remarried by then and not around. But then, Taryn hadn't been around, either, and she looked like she wanted to cry just thinking about it. "Why did she mean so much to you? You'd never even met her beyond the few hours we were backstage together. Was it just that her music spoke to you as a kid?"

She shook her head, blinking back what appeared to be honest-to-goodness tears. "I respected her for what she'd done, where she came from. Nobody ever believed in her—at least, before you came along—but she still made it. She came out on top. That takes guts."

"And you can relate to that, nobody believing in you? Nobody but Sarah and me, that is?"

She blinked again, this time to clear the emotion it seemed, as when she once again looked at him, her gaze was vacant.

Taryn let out a long, loud yawn that was overdone even before she stood and added in a lengthy stretch. She glanced over to the bedroom area at the alarm clock. "Wow, it's late. I should go."

She should, before he pressed her for more answers, or started giving answers of his own that he hadn't shared in three long years. Never to anyone who wasn't related.

Brian opened his mouth to agree, but instead said, "You could. Or you could stay."

Caution filled her eyes. "I'm not sleeping with you again. We don't work together, not when push comes to shove."

They could work together. They would. At least, in the physical way she meant. He hadn't asked her to stay for physical reasons, though. He'd asked her to stay because he didn't feel like being alone at the moment. Which was odd, because he valued his solitude more than anything else.

He forced a laugh. "Push comes to shove—that's quite the visual. And I'd have to disagree about us not working together. You just haven't given us a real chance. Yet."

Taryn's eyebrows danced together in a familiar scowl. "Then we'll have to agree to disagree, because there isn't going to be a yet." Her tone softened. "Good night, Brian. Thanks for the ice cream, and...everything."

"Night."

He intended to let her go at that, just one simple word, but then he found himself following her to the door. And when she opened it and darted a glance in both directions down the long hallway, he found himself grabbing her arm and swinging her back around.

The breath left her mouth in an audible *whoosh* as she slammed into his chest. Her eyes were wide as he took possession of her mouth. For an instant, she was still. Then her hands came to his shoulders, and her fingers curled into the cotton of his T-shirt. Her tongue was explosive, thrusting, darting, licking at his.

She was being dominant again. Brian nearly laughed. Only laughing would get him the same place telling her how good taking things slow could be— absolutely nowhere. Showing was what she needed.

He pushed against her tongue with his, forcing it out of his mouth. When it was back in her mouth, he retracted his, as well, and brushed her lips. She murmured and tried to push her tongue against his mouth. He caught it in his teeth and nipped lightly. With a squeak, she pulled it back between her lips.

Holding her loosely, so that she could feel his erection, but not do anything about it, he nibbled at the corners of her lips. Slowly, he traced the soft contours with his tongue, moistening the sensitive flesh. Taryn whimpered and tried to deepen the kiss. He slowed things down again, kissing her with soft brushes of lips against lips, featherlight caresses. She seemed to get the message this time and didn't try to rush things, and he rewarded her by giving her back his tongue.

He pushed between her lips with purpose, stroked the silken heat of her mouth from roof to floor, side to side, then finally gave her what he knew she wanted and rubbed his tongue against hers.

With that rub, she seemed to get the idea it was okay to move again. Her hands traveled down his shoulders and back to grasp his ass. Brian knew she would try to take things over next, probably start by returning his earlier swats. Before she could go wild, he did.

Dragging her firmly to him, he ground his solid cock against her belly while his tongue swirled and danced and fondled hers with greedy strokes and sucks and licks. He ate at her mouth, pushed his hips against hers, until her nails pressed into his butt through his shorts, and she cried out against his mouth. And then he removed his mouth from hers, let her go, and stepped back.

Her black hair floated in righteous indignation around her flushed face, and her mouth looked well loved. Taking in the overall picture, though, Taryn just looked plain stunned.

As he'd done earlier this night, Brian stepped back into the room and shut the door, so that only a fraction of her face was visible. "Since you already said you wouldn't stay, I suggest you get moving before someone catches you standing outside my room, swollen-lipped and breathing hard," he said, then closed the door on the woman who was quickly becoming his favorite to tease and the one he wanted to fuck so badly he'd be lucky to sleep tonight.

Chapter Twelve

"They make me wish I had someone to bring to Sugar Foot."

Taryn followed Dawn's gaze to the laughing couple seated less than an inch apart at a table on the other side of the restaurant's open courtyard. Dawn had been in the same late-morning workshop as Taryn, and when it ended, they'd agreed to find somewhere to go for lunch. Then, whether Dawn wanted to get distance from the conference the way that Taryn did—okay, so for Taryn it was a specific person—or for some other reason, the blonde had suggested they find a place on the other side of the island.

They'd chosen this restaurant by the takeout menu Taryn had picked up from a brochure kiosk in the Seaside's lobby. She hadn't realized until they stepped off the island shuttle that the place was across the road from the beach she'd gone to for relaxing shade-time yesterday only to end up getting an eyeful. As explicit as things had gotten between Snake Guy and his brunette lover, it was amazing she hadn't dreamed about them.

Then again, in order to dream about the exhibitionist couple, she would have to move past thoughts of Brian. And that seemed a damned impossible feat.

The man had gone well beyond having her confused. Now she was just plain clueless.

Was he not the corporate shark and all-around jerk she'd rendered in her mind, but truly a nice guy? Had it been nothing more than a show to ignite her passion when he'd trapped her against the entertainment center and taunted her with his wicked actions and arrogant words? And if it had been a show, why, after sharing a friendly conversation, did he have to ruin it by kissing her good night and shutting the door in her face? For the second time.

Ugh. Men!

"Either that, or they make me want to be ill," Dawn said, when the couple across the way stood and gave in to a lingering kiss before making their way, hand in hand, to the restaurant's exit.

The man wore no shirt. He'd been sitting with his back to Taryn before, and the chair had hidden that fact. Given the laid-back lifestyle on the island, to be shirtless while dining in the courtyard wasn't a big shock. The unforgettable dark and deadly looking black snake on the man's back, however, was a surprise. Yesterday Snake Guy had been with a diminutive brunette. Today his giggling companion was a curvaceous redhead.

It shouldn't faze her. She didn't even know the guy. So he got around, so what. She got around too—at least when her lucky-count streak was running a bit smoother, and thoughts of Brian weren't plaguing her night and day.

Ick. Back to Brian.

Snake Guy and his redheaded friend disappeared from sight. For a moment longer, Taryn wondered over the man and what it was about him that bothered her. She dismissed it then to laugh at Dawn's words. "Such a fine line there, between jealousy and wanting to puke. So, I take it that means you aren't married?"

"Not anymore." Dawn lifted her iced tea in the air, as if saluting her freedom. She brought the glass to her mouth and took a long drink before responding. "Jeff had his priorities screwed up. Basically they were his boat, his dog, and then me."

"Eeuw. Sorry to hear that, but it sounds like leaving him was the right thing to do."

"Actually, he left me when he added a younger woman to the top of that list of priorities. And I do mean young—fresh out of high school." Taryn's disgust must have showed, as the other woman laughed softly. "It was upsetting at first, but that was a couple years ago. Now I'm enjoying the single life. If nothing else, it gives me a chance to focus on my songwriting."

"That is a plus."

Dawn's smile fell, and she said soberly, "It's nice, but honestly there are times I consider marrying again if I find the right man. Jeff acted like my songwriting was a joke. I don't want that again. What about you?"

What about her? Did she want someone who believed in her songwriting? Yes, Taryn knew without having to think about it. Outside of Sarah, she hadn't had anyone who ever really believed in her. And Brian...wouldn't be in her life after Sunday. As far as marriage went... "I've never come close to marrying, but maybe some day if, like you said, I find someone who returns my love and believes in my songwriting."

"Do your friends believe in you?"

"Some do." Okay, one friend did. Unless she counted Brian as a friend. And he would be gone in a few days, and she also still wasn't sure which side of the nice guy fence he fell on, Taryn didn't. He was just a...guy she was using for free ice cream, songwriting help, and sex.

Scratch that last one. She wasn't using him for sex. They weren't having sex. Never had good sex. Well not good sex that involved consummation. They'd had good sex without consummation. And she hadn't exactly been strapped down then. Yeah, she'd been tired that first time and, well, rising to a stupid challenge the second time, but she'd been the one in control. Not in an aggressive control-freak way, either, but in a moderated control way, where they were sharing the power.

Yep, they'd had a nice equal power thing happening both those times.

And if she sat here and thought about sex—fully consummated or otherwise—with Brian for another second, Taryn would scream.

"I think it's the kind of thing only another person in the business can understand," Dawn said. "My folks act like they get it, but I know they really don't. Is your family supportive?"

Now there was a much better topic than Brian. Her family. Her loving parents who adored her songwriting and had supported her dreams since she was a young girl. Yeah, maybe in some perpendicular universe.

In the four short days they'd been on this island, Brian had shown more interest in her songwriting than her parents ever had. He'd acted like he cared. Like he was sincere when he said how much he believed in her. He seemed just as sincere when he claimed to be good in bed; only when he spoke those words his expression was ruled with passion. And, damn it, that passion had really started to speak to her.

That kiss he'd stunned her with last night had been thick with it. Not hurried passion, but a slow, sensual building passion that suddenly erupted and...and, good grief, she was growing damp just thinking about erupting passion.

"Shoot, here comes the waiter," Dawn said, saving Taryn from having to respond to her question. The blonde opened her menu and looked down at it. "Guess I'd better stop yapping and decide what I want."

"Yeah, I'd say that makes two of us." Only Taryn knew, even as she said the words, the want in question in her mind had nothing to do with food.

Twenty minutes later, Taryn was halfway through her island berry chicken salad. The conversation had turned to talk of what they'd hoped to find time to do during nonconference hours. Much to Taryn's delight, she'd learned that Dawn loved to dance and hadn't been out to a club in months. They'd agreed to go out Friday night, and Taryn was already planning all the naughty things she'd do with the guy after she picked out her island hottie.

She'd said she wouldn't spend any more time on this island partaking in pleasure now that the conference had started, but the last while had made her realize how important pleasure was. Her twisted mind kept thinking back to if she might want to sleep with Brian again. Part of her had even become convinced that she couldn't shake thoughts of him from her head. Now she knew better. Now she knew her want was based on horniness alone. The burning need to feel something hot and hard between her legs.

Really any man would do, so long as he was anatomically correct. Okay, so she hadn't given eunuchs a try, but the pleasure factor there just didn't seem too likely. Really, a tongue could only reach so far.

Mulling over the dynamics of that thought, Taryn forked a large bite of salad into her mouth.

"I'd like to get my hands on Brian Macovney," a woman's voice came from behind her. "Talk about a hot bod."

"I heard he's explosive in bed," a second female voice chirped in.

Taryn's jaw locked on a gasp, and the bite slid down her throat before she could attempt to chew it. She inhaled on a painful breath. Tears clouded her eyes. She could feel the poky leaves of the lettuce, the serrated edges of the carrots, and those astonishingly sweet little red island berries brushing her windpipe. They tickled, damn it, they tickled.

She fought the urge to giggle. This wasn't funny. She was going to die of salad asphyxiation over a lie about Brian's potency.

There! If that wasn't proof he wasn't a nice guy, what was? He was going to kill her, the bastard!

Dawn's eyes widened with concern. "You okay?"

Yeah, she was just great, probably turning blue by now. Maybe she should move to the ground, that way when she keeled over, she wouldn't fall out of her chair and make a huge scene by cracking her head open and spilling out its contents. People were eating, after all.

"Drink, Taryn!" Dawn stood and thrust a glass of water into her hand.

When Taryn didn't move to lift the glass to her lips, Dawn put it there and tipped it back. Taryn drank automatically. The first cool splash of water on her throat was chilling, then added to the tickling sensation of the lettuce and carrots and those damned sweet little berries. Slowly, the tickling faded and her common sense returned, along with the reality of her predicament.

With a bursting cough, Taryn pushed the water glass aside and slapped at her chest. The breath screamed from her lungs in hitching gasps. People were looking at her.

No, everyone was looking at her, Taryn realized when her breathing was almost back to normal, and she was able to glance around.

Their server, a dimpled guy who looked closer to his teens than his twenties, appeared at the table. He shifted from foot to foot, as if he was worried about having to do the Heimlich on her. "Ma'am, are you okay?"

"I...I'm fine." She sounded like a frog. Lovely. So much for finding an island hottie with this voice. Not that she needed an island hottie when Brian was clearly all he said and more.

The server gave her a last worried look, and then, when she once more assured him she was fine, left the table. Disbelief pushing through her mind, Taryn turned in her chair to take in the women she'd heard speaking before. The pair must be from the conference, though they didn't look familiar. She wanted to go over there and set them straight. Only doing that would allude to the fact that she'd slept with Brian, and she wouldn't make that known.

Taryn turned back to her salad and with a, "What? I'm fine," to those diners still watching, stuffed another bite in her mouth. This time, she was extra careful to chew slowly while she listened to the conversation behind her.

The women spoke about Brian for a few more minutes, nothing worthwhile, just verbally drooling like a couple of high schoolers, and then changed the topic.

As soon as Dawn went off to find the restroom, Taryn changed that topic right back for them. She had to do it, to set the poor women's facts straight.

Putting on what she hoped was an *I just want to warn you, I don't really care about him* face, she pulled a chair up to the table and sat down. The women stopped chatting to look at her. "I don't normally eavesdrop," Taryn said, before they could question her move, "but I heard you talking about Brian

Macovney's, uh, bedside manner earlier, and I'm curious who your source is."

"The woman I sat next to in this morning's workshop on demo techniques," the bleached blonde on Taryn's right said.

Taryn quickly identified her as the one who'd said she wanted to get with Brian. Given the way she was dressed—a cleavage-hugging tank top and tiny shorts—and that she had the body to fill those clothes, she probably *could* get with Brian with little effort at all.

Before the night was through he would be doing her, probably on the balcony just to tick Taryn off. "I wouldn't believe everything you hear."

Blondie lifted a shoulder. "She seemed like she knew him pretty well. She said how relieved she was to see him happy again, because he'd been so upset right after his mother's death and still seemed to be taking it hard the last few years."

So it wasn't Blondie she had to worry about. It was this other woman. This woman who was close enough with Brian he spoke about his mother to her. A prickly sensation Taryn hated to acknowledge as jealousy pushed through her. Trying and failing to keep the snark from her voice, she asked, "Does this woman have a name?"

"Serena, I believe she said. Honestly, I've met so many people the last couple of days, I could be way off." Blondie's gaze turned knowing. "Word to the wise, if you plan on asking her if his performance lives up to his appearance, you'd be a heck of a lot better off finding out for yourself."

Yeah, like Blondie knew her so well after thirty seconds, she could guess why Taryn was asking about Brian. *I think not!* "He's not my type."

"Honey, he's hot, rich, and has a bedroom reputation that precedes him—he's every woman's type."

"More like fantasy," Blondie's friend piped in with a giggle.

Taryn really wanted to say something about how wrong it was that these women sat around fantasizing about Brian like he was nothing more than a piece of meat to use and discard, but just then Dawn stepped back out on the courtyard. With a "thanks" to the women, she put back the chair and returned to their table.

"Are they from the conference?" Dawn asked as she sat.

Taryn shook her head. "Nah, they were just curious what kind of salad I had. I guess they saw me turning blue and decided they didn't want to order it."

Chapter Thirteen

"Do you know Serena?" Taryn's question barreled through Brian's door, ruling out the idea she'd come to his room for further songwriting inspiration.

Her irritable expression as he let her into his room and closed the door also ruled out his hope to not think about Serena. The woman had been a conference liaison and workshop moderator for as long as Brian had been attending the event. That first year they'd hit it off after one too many drinks during the end of the week contract award party. The night had ended with them breathing hard and tangled in the sheets. Since Serena lived less than an hour's drive from his Knoxville home, the relationship had continued after they left the island, and at some point became about more than sex. Then Brian's mother had taken sick, and Serena had just...

Hell, Serena hadn't done a damned thing.

During those long, painful months as his mother tried to hide her disease from the public eye and continue with her stage career, Brian had figured out how much more he wanted out of a woman than Serena could give him. Thanks to his shitty attitude at the time, things ended messily between them. Still, when the next year's conference rolled around, Serena wanted to reconcile for no-strings-attached sex following the contract award party. Against his better judgment, he'd given in, then repeated the same dick-driven mistake last year.

This morning Serena approached him with that knowing look in her eyes and smiled in the coy way that used to make his cock swell on sight. He'd neither gotten hard nor accepted her offer. She'd taken it well, giving him a soft pout and then an understanding smile. Brian hadn't taken it nearly as well. Mainly because he knew why he'd turned her down, and that reason was standing in front of him, looking pissed as hell.

Had Serena approached Taryn?

No. Serena could be somewhat wild in bed with the right persuasion, but she wasn't aggressive enough to go after a man who'd rejected her.

Serena wasn't like Taryn at all. And that's exactly why Brian should have accepted the other woman's offer. He didn't want to deal with dominance outside of his business dealings—even if her aggressive side was mostly a farce. And where did Taryn get off acting so mad anyway? They weren't an item. They weren't even sleeping together.

Unless that was why she'd come. To tell him she'd changed her mind about not wanting him.

Hope cruised through Brian with a force of concerning proportions. He went to the table where he'd been typing notes on the conference attendees he'd interviewed and those he'd met in passing. He sat and closed the laptop, then looked back at Taryn. "I'm afraid I'm going to need a little more information than that," he said, purposely sounding bored.

Taryn crossed the room and, hands on the hips of a knee-length brown skirt, eyed him down hard. "She claims to have slept with you around the time your mom passed away. She said you're explosive in bed." Her hard look relented, and she snorted. "I don't even know why I listened to such an obvious lie. I mean Quick to the finish Willy explosive. Yeah right."

Too many times she'd taken a crack at his staying power. One too many to sit here and act like he didn't give a shit what she thought.

Tension bunched his muscles and pushed at his temples. Brian shot to his feet until they were standing nearly toe-to-toe. Today she wore casual brown pumps that allowed his height a towering advantage. Pumps that looked completely out of place on someone so alluring. Taryn, of the striking blue eyes, luscious, thick black hair and too-damned-kissable mouth, belonged in those fuck-me heels she'd worn the other night. Right along with that seductive, siren red dress. The way that thing thrust her big breasts in his face, barely covered her delectable ass...

His dick had been solid from the second she opened her door. Swollen and aching to plow inside her willing, wet body, just as it was now.

Annoyed that Taryn could affect him so easily when safe, submissive Serena hadn't been able to register any interest at all, Brian bit out, "Willy isn't his name, and Serena wasn't lying."

"You *do* know her," Taryn accused. "Have you seen her lately?"

"Define lately."

"Since you arrived on Sugar Foot?"

"She's here?" he asked, hoping to learn how it was that Taryn had happened to not only have met Serena, but spoke with her about their physical history.

"From what I understand, she is."

In other words, she heard the information through a second party. Some of the tension left Brian's body, along with a few degrees of his building temper.

"Was she your girlfriend?"

The rest of the tension left him with the aversion that filled Taryn's voice. It should have bothered him when the reason for her behavior reached him; instead he could only let go the rest of his temper to laugh. "You're jealous."

She huffed. "Hardly."

"Then why do you look like you're torn between kissing me and killing me?"

Honestly, she looked more like she wanted to kill him without any kissing involved. Now that he'd laid the idea out there, though, that changed. Her gaze went to his mouth and her throat worked visibly as she swiped the damp tip of her tongue across her full lower lip.

Feeling a little dry-mouthed, was she?

Brian grinned as he concentrated on her slightly parted lips, let his look reflect the primal hunger that had been chasing through him for far too long now. From the moment he'd first set eyes on her again this past Sunday to be exact. It was time to fulfill that hunger, and none too soon, either.

Slowly, he leaned toward her, waiting to see if she'd back down, step away, become the Taryn filled with insecurity and hesitation.

She didn't back down or step away, only whispered, "I don't want to kiss you," and gave her lips another lick, this one long and lusty.

Thoughts of other places she might stroke that talented tongue of hers had his heart picking up while his cock gave an impatient throb. "Are you sure, because it looks like you do?"

"I'm sure I want to kiss you."

The response wasn't a whisper this time, but a loud and clear announcement that rang with desire and told him exactly what part of Taryn he was dealing with. The aggressive one that would never back down. She would cast away her controlling side and give in to his commands, though. With just a little bit of persuasion, she would.

Brian lifted her hands from her hips and pulled her to him until her body was all but flush with his. He lowered his head and threaded a hand through her hair to expose her ear. Just that move was enough to ignite a shiver in Taryn.

She blinked at him. Once. Twice. Her pupils dilated. "Take me" was written in her suddenly stormy blue eyes; the urgent silent demand reflected in her quickened breathing and the flushing of her cheeks.

"I thought you said you didn't want to kiss me?"

"Yeah, well, I'm a woman and that gives me two prerogatives. One, to change my mind, and, two, to roar."

"Ro—"

The question died on his lips as she rose on tiptoe and slanted her glistening mouth against his. Brian had the momentary thought he'd walked right into her trap, and then forgot all about it as her arms snaked around his middle and her tongue pushed into his mouth.

She sent his senses reeling with fast, demanding sucks and soft, needful moans while her hands roamed over his back, rubbing, squeezing, then falling to his ass to cup and pinch. The pinching hurt. Almost.

He'd doled out his share of painful pressure, but rarely had been on the receiving end. The jolts of raw burning pleasure shooting from his butt to his groin, tightening his balls along the way, suggested he might not mind giving Taryn the control. Right after he pinched and paddled her ass a couple dozen times.

With the ultimate goal of baring her backside and most every other inch of her fine flesh, he wrenched the plain-Jane blouse from the drab skirt. The underwire of her bra barely paused him as he pushed beneath to fill his hands with the generous mounds of her breasts. Her skin was soft against his palms. Soft and hot, and soon to be wet.

The feasting of Taryn's mouth continued while her grip on his ass let up. He'd changed into shorts and a T-shirt following the conference dinner, and she took advantage of the easy access his loose-fitting clothing granted. Shoving her hand inside his shorts and past his briefs, she fisted his cock. With each pump of her hand, she rubbed her breasts against his palms, taunting his flesh with the hardened peaks of her nipples.

Brian grunted against her lips with each of those pumps, sighed at the erotic bliss rocketing through him, snugging his balls with his building release.

The woman was going too damned fast again, trying to kill his attempts at persuasion. If she didn't stop soon, she wouldn't get what she wanted. Neither of them would. No matter how wickedly good her hand felt wrapped around his cock, he would not let things end on an abrupt and disappointing note.

He pulled his mouth from hers. "Taryn, stop."

"Nuh-uh." The glide of her hand continued. Her hips joined in, pivoting against his crotch, rocking their pelvises together while her mouth went to work on his neck. She murmured in between nibbles, "Don't want to. Gotta keep going. Hot."

Not hot enough. Not even close. This time neither of them was coming until they were both on the edge of carnal madness. Wrapping his fingers around hers, he lifted her hand from his shorts. "Stop now, or I'm throwing you out of this room!"

With a squeak of annoyance, she pulled her mouth from his neck, her hand from his, and stepped back. Frustration shone in her eyes. "Fine. I stopped."

Yeah, but she was practically vibrating with the need to start again. He was too. That didn't change the way this thing was going to play out. Regardless of who was in control, this would not be a fast, hasty fuck. He owed her something far better than that. He wanted something far better than that too, for his own selfish reasons.

Brian offered his hand. "If we're going to do this, then we're going to do it right, so that we both end up satisfied. Agreed?"

A moment's uncertainty crossed Taryn's face, and then she nodded and took his hand. "Yes. I want that. I want you to prove to me that you're being sincere when you say you know how to push a woman's pleasure buttons. I want to see this sexual deity you claim to be."

He grinned. "Is that another of your challenges, Taryn? Because if it is, I guarantee I can live up to it. Trust me, woman, let me take the lead for a few minutes and I'll have you coming so hard you scream."

Excitement chased through her eyes. Before she could respond, he pulled her toward the bed. He stopped near the bedside end table, long enough to grab a condom from the package he'd placed in the drawer and pocket it, then continued through the room.

"Where are we going?" Taryn asked.

"To the balcony."

"The balcony?"

With a nod, he glanced at her. "The other night I ruined your fantasy; now I plan to fix it."

"That's...nice of you," she said as they stepped out onto the balcony and into the late-afternoon sun. "And unexpected."

He laughed at her knit brow, the fact she seemed almost speechless. "Still confusing you, am I?"

"Maybe. Maybe no—"

Brian grabbed her around the waist and lifted her onto the balcony railing before she could finish her sentence. Taryn's eyes widened. She tried to scramble back off the railing and onto the balcony floor. He moved between her thighs and grabbed her wrists, held them both to him with one hand, while he moved his other hand beneath her skirt.

The material had crept up, and from this angle, the skirt didn't look so drab. Matter of fact, it looked pretty damned fine. He slid his hand higher, smiling when he found the damp crotch of her panties. He stroked her slit through the wet material, eager to part the folds and uncover the hot pussy beneath. "Scared?

"No." She shifted her hips with each caress. "It's just that—"

"At your room, we were one story up, at mine we're eight? Don't worry, I won't let you go." Brian wouldn't, either, because as long as he held Taryn's wrists in his hands, there was no way she could take over the control.

Chapter Fourteen

Nice guy. Ooohhh...yum...Brian was a nice guy.

And for the second time this week, Taryn was burning up.

Only this time it wasn't because her skin was fried to a crisp. This time the inferno of heat came from the inside, starting from between the juncture of her thighs, where he teased her clit through her panties.

She was so wet. Dripping for him.

She wanted to be out of these clothes. Now. Wanted to feel him impaling her, taking her deep and making her scream the way he promised.

But he said that wouldn't happen if she moved too fast, and so she had to be patient, because she *would* have everything Serena had had.

Only she didn't want everything Serena had, Taryn reminded herself. Brian hadn't admitted that Serena had been his girlfriend, and everyone knew you avoided questions you would have to lie to answer the way someone else wanted to hear them. Which meant Serena *had* been his girlfriend.

Taryn didn't want to be his girlfriend, or even his friend. Not for more than the next few days anyway.

Maybe the next few days they could be friends. Friends who... "Oh, God!"

Her thoughts came to a screeching halt when Brian's finger stopped the teasing to push beneath her panties and deep inside her slick pussy. The breath whooshed out of her as he withdrew his finger and tugged her off the railing.

He'd told her that he wouldn't let her go. Up until this moment, she hadn't considered the meaning of those words.

Did he intend to keep her hands bound in one of his until they were finished? He'd told her several times how good being submissive could feel, had played some sort of control game when he'd claimed to be instilling passion in her and then again when he'd kissed her last night. His intentions now had to be more than a game. He had to be after complete possession of her.

Brian hauled her in front of him and grabbed the hem of her skirt. "I want you out of this."

He dragged the skirt up slowly, the slide of the cool inner lining against her skin a sensual delight she couldn't stop from shivering over. That shiver grew to a tremble when the skirt was bunched at her waist and he hooked a finger under the side strap of the barely there panties she'd worn in opposition to her formal outerwear.

"Out of these too. Out of everything." He tipped back his head, and his eyes flashed intensely green and full of command. "Naked, Taryn—that's how you're going to be for me, aren't you?"

Taryn's inner voice shouted a vehement no. Normally she didn't like to be ruled this way—whether he believed it or not, when it came to sex she was all about equality and giving as good as she got. Normally she didn't want a man taking possession of her. Normally she didn't want that. But she also didn't normally perch on the edge of an eighth-story balcony with only Brian's hands to stabilize her.

The moment's panic she'd experienced when he'd first placed her on the railing had been well worth the ensuing rush of excitement as the push of the muggy evening breeze and the crash of the growing tide caught up with her. She hadn't been scared then. She hadn't because he was hanging on to her, and for whatever twisted reason, she'd trusted him. Now she trusted him, as well. She also felt more of that secret thrill licking through her, stoking a burning fire of need.

No, normally, Taryn didn't like to be ruled, but now she did. Now she ached to hear his rough commands. To experience his forceful handling. "Strip me. I don't have any hands, so take my clothes off. Now!"

"Is that an order?"

"Yes." She flinched the second the word left her mouth, aware it was the wrong answer.

A whack of his palm to her ass confirmed her speculation. A whack that, like everything else Brian was doing to her, only intensified her excitement. Her pussy creamed with anticipation, and her butt tingled for more of the same. Only with her panties off. And on his schedule, of course.

"It wasn't an order. I was asking you to strip me. I want to be naked for you."

His mouth tilted in a sexy half grin. "Then beg."

Taryn bit her lip while her belly tightened. "That's too demeaning, Brian. I can't do it."

He crooked an eyebrow while his hands moved up her inner thighs, teasingly slow, only to stop centimeters from her pulsing sex. One finger moved toward the center of her panties. Not touching, just lingering there so close...so damned close. The finger moved the tiniest bit closer, and her breath caught at the rush of liquid desire that welled within her cunt.

Brian's grin deepened. "You sure?"

"Yes." She just couldn't beg. It was so far beyond her principles, her limits.

In one fluid move, his hovering finger pushed past her panties, parted her labia, and touched down on her clit. A single firm stroke of the bundle of nerves proved she was neither as principle-bound nor as limited as she'd believed. Another stroke had her realizing she might not have any principles at all. The third stroke assured she didn't have so much as a fraction of logic left.

"Not sure." She panted, squirming as the strokes continued, the pressure of his finger increased. "Might beg."

Taryn struggled to steal her hands from his grasp. She longed to tear off his T-shirt, followed by his shorts and briefs. She yearned to get him gloriously naked. His toned, tanned, succulent body bared. She ached to lick him from head to toe.

But all she was doing was racing.

Her mind. Her heart. Her inner muscles clamping a little more with each caress.

Brian knew what he was doing. He knew *exactly* what he was doing.

Her heart feeling ready to pound out of her chest a little more with each erratic beat, she tipped back her head and stared up at the overhead balcony. She could only see the floor of it, but it was clear anyone above them could see them looking down. A glance in either direction revealed no one, but that didn't mean they weren't there, watching.

The idea they could have voyeurs kicked aside any lingering reservations about begging. She wanted Brian. Wanted his cock buried inside her, now. If that wouldn't happen until she begged, then to hell with it. "Please. Please strip me."

"If that's what you want, Taryn," he said lazily, as if his heart wasn't exploding inside his chest, his body hard as flint. His heart had to be galloping, his cock ready to erupt. It had to be, because this was Brian— quick to the finish Brian—who had no staying power.

Unless Serena had been accurate. Unless Brian had been sincere. Unless he could be a regular Energizer bunny and keep going and going and going.

Before Taryn could see his expression, he removed his finger from her panties and turned her around. The rasping of the zipper as he lowered her skirt sounded even louder than her madly throbbing heart. The skirt slipped leisurely down her legs, igniting every nerve ending in her thighs and ass not already making a standing ovation.

The hunger in his thick voice as he spoke ignited every other, still dormant, cell in her body. "What next?"

Everything. Only she knew he wouldn't go that fast. "Panties. Panties next."

Her panties were whispering down her legs in a blink. She kicked off her too-sensible shoes, then stepped out of the panties and skirt. Anticipating his next move, she prepared to be turned back around. Instead he swatted her ass, hard.

Taryn yelped and grabbed hold of the railing's wrought iron. Wicked sensation rioted through her body, teased stinging heat over her butt, and trickled juices down her inner thighs.

His palm fell across her backside a second time, and he warned, "Next time don't forget the please."

She bucked back against his hand, all but asking for a third helping. Like hell she would say please. Not unless it was pleading for another decadent swat.

When his fingers found her again, it wasn't to paddle but turn her back toward him. Lust smoldered in his eyes. Eyes that were no longer in the vicinity of her own, but almost even with her crotch. Instantly, his mouth was on her sex, a day's growth of stubble tickling her lips as he loved her labia with a casual flick of his tongue that couldn't feel any less casual.

He pulled his head back to reveal that sexy-as-sin grin. More potent than ever because his lips shimmered erotically with her juices. "Tasty. Now what?"

"More of that." Lots more. Lots deeper too. "Please."

The flat of his hand fell between her legs this time. A gently stinging swat that consumed her pussy with electric sensation.

He made a tsking sound, while his eyes showed amusement. "Clothing, Taryn. Think clothing." He rocked back on his heels to finger the button of her blouse centered directly between her breasts. "Do we go for the shirt next, or do you think we should leave that on? The way the wind's blowing, if we took off your bra next, the material would rub against your nipples." He moved his fingers across her shirt, over a nipple. "Get them all hot and hard." He rubbed at the already achingly hot and hard peak. "You'd be begging me all over again, just so I would suck on them." His hand left her breast, and he flickered his gaze to her sex. "Or maybe you'd want me to suck on something a little lower. Give the neighbors a vacation show to remember."

Her sex contracted with his hot look and the idea any number of people were eyeing her bared body, waiting with shared anticipation of Brian's next move. A swat. A lick. A fuck. Any of them would do. Anything but stopping. "Bra. Leave the shirt on. Please."

Leaving the top two buttons of her shirt fastened, he made quick work of removing her bra. He stood back then, as far as his grip on her hands would allow, and traveled his gaze the length of her. A low whistle confirmed he liked what he saw, despite the shaking of his head. "Not bad. But I want more. Spread your legs. Let me get a good look at that pussy."

Wanting to please him now almost as badly as she wanted to find lasting pleasure at his hands, Taryn opened her stance. The breeze licked salaciously between her thighs, a warm whisper along her hairless mound, and minitremors quaked through her sex.

Tremors that grew exponentially with the appreciative smacking of Brian's lips. "Better. I still want more." Keeping his gaze locked on her crotch, he freed her hands. "Pull your lips apart. Let me see that clit."

The raw ecstasy clinging to his voice, overtaking his features seduced her to the point of no hesitation. One hand moved to her labia, spreading the lips wide, exposing the nub within. The nub that throbbed for contact. She clenched her pussy to waylay the ache, stop her other hand from journeying between her legs in an effort to relief some of the madly building pressure.

Brian's smile was pure male arrogance and knowing. "You want to touch yourself, don't you?" He didn't wait for a response, but gifted her with his approval. "Go ahead. Touch. Tease. Finger." He moved to her side and leaned back against the railing. "I'll just sit here and watch."

Without pause, Taryn allowed her free hand to dart between her legs. She thumbed her clit, and from that first touch, the blood sizzled through her on a dead-center voyage to the engorged nub. Spreading her lips wider, she captured her clit between thumb and forefinger and squeezed hard. She cried out with the sharp contact, and her pussy convulsed with a flood of juices.

She couldn't resist the urge to thrust her fingers inside, couldn't stop the pistoning of her hips as she rode two fingers to the knuckles. Her clit scraped across the bone. Eyes falling shut, she whimpered with the awesome pressure. "So good. So, *sooo* good."

Never had she been this amazingly aroused, by a man's hands or her own. She needed release, like now.

"Now that's nice. You have a beautiful cunt. All pink and juicy. Should I get my camera? Can I take pictures of you fucking yourself, Taryn?"

Taryn's eyes snapped open. She'd almost forgotten she had an audience. Almost managed to forget time and place completely. The all-out admiration in Brian's eyes wouldn't allow her to forget a second longer. She wanted to fuck him so badly she hurt with the need, and yet she wanted to kiss him even more. "You can. Or you can kiss me."

Surprise at her request showed in his eyes. And then it was gone as he pulled her into his arms, slanted his mouth against hers, and met her tongue with the urgent stroke of his own.

The taste of him exploded in her mouth, the scent of his skin, his arousal over her senses. He tasted of desperation, of holding himself back. And then he added her flavor to the mix, by lifting her juice-slicked fingers to his lips and licking them clean. He returned his mouth to hers, and the sexy taste of her cream stretched her control to the snapping point.

She'd been good. She'd been patient. She wanted her reward.

"Now I want you naked." Taryn half pleaded, half demanded.

And now he must want that same thing, because Brian responded instantly. Yanking the T-shirt over his head to reveal a suntanned chest, ripe with glistening muscle and sinew that had her salivating like a schoolgirl.

Too fast. They were going too fast again.

Brian knew it even as he pushed his shorts and briefs down his legs, all the while keeping his gaze trained on Taryn's face. That she was more than ready to topple over the edge and into orgasm made going too fast okay.

Between her voracious look and the way her hands were curling and uncurling at her sides, she looked like she wanted to jump him again, the way she had last time they'd been on a balcony together. Before she got any crazy ideas of doing just that, he grabbed the condom from his shorts pocket, quickly rolled it on, and did the jumping himself.

Pulling Taryn into his arms, he lifted her up his body and once more took hold of that sinful mouth of hers. She wrapped her legs around his waist, and her hot, wet opening pressed against his cock. Perspiration beaded his forehead; a trickle of it moved along his spine. Not an effect of the muggy night, but rather his hot-as-hell companion.

The woman was like the greatest aphrodisiac. From the moment he'd skimmed the ugly skirt down her shapely legs, he'd wanted his dick buried inside her. He'd told her that he'd live up to her sexual-deity expectations, but he'd been ready to blow it right then and there. Watching her finger herself had been a lesson in control of monumental proportions. Licking the cream of her labor from her fingers was damned near his undoing.

The important thing was that he hadn't come undone, and he wouldn't until she was ready to go along for the ride.

Cupping the soft globes of her ass, Brian rocked the length of his dick along her slit. With the long-drawn-out moan of a sexually starved woman, she rocked back and dug her nails into his skin. The nip was hard, urgent, commanding, the way he hadn't let her be while under his control. It made clear without words exactly how much she needed him inside her. The juices trickling from her pussy amplified that fact while sending his need soaring.

He moved his mouth to her neck, to that spot that always drove her wild. With first a lick and then a teasing whisper of hot breath, he slipped a finger inside her from behind.

"Good." Taryn sighed. "Better," she added when he moved his lips to layer love bites on her neck, beneath her ear, along the tender lobe.

While his mouth feasted, his fingers stroked, from perineum to clit to slit and back again. He took his fingers higher, toyed with the opening of her asshole, and the breath puffed from her lips in hot, hasty pants. Her fingernails dug into his back. Her hips bumped wildly, nearly stealing his fingers from his prize.

Brian sighed his thanksgiving. She was ready for him, and he was past the point of ready for her. Filling his hands with the roundness of her ass, he took her lips with his. Devoured the slightly too wide lower one, then the top one, and then he met her stormy blue eyes and drove his cock deep within the wet, welcoming warmth of her pussy.

Taryn's mouth ripped from his to shout an ecstatic, "Yes! Thank you!" that echoed off the balcony walls and, no doubt, throughout most of the island.

And as she moved against him, riding him with triumphant abandon, Brian mimicked that exuberant shout with one of his own.

She stroked her hands over his back, down along his spine, to the swell of his ass, and then returned to ply more of that salacious nipping of her nails into his shoulders. Her mouth was like wildfire, suckling, foraging, consuming him whole. Pumping into her with thrusts positioned for maximum pleasure, he consumed her back, tangled his tongue with hers and savored her hot, sweet taste.

Another shout was building inside him, one he knew would be accompanied by climax. Relief and euphoria poured through him with the clamping of her cunt around his cock, and she broke from his mouth to let loose a rapturous cry as she came. The tremors from her quaking body tackled the last of his control. Burying his face against her chest, he gave in to orgasm with a growl.

Chapter Fifteen

What Brian had done to Taryn on his hotel room balcony this afternoon hadn't been her fantasy. It had been even better. As had what he did to her a short while after that, in the comfort of his queen-size bed.

It had been harrowing to admit he'd been right; he knew exactly what buttons to push to have her climaxing so hard she was liable to dream about that moment for the rest of her days. It was still somewhat harrowing over an hour later as they sat in Maria's Cantina on the other side of the island.

They should be at an evening seminar right now—her listening, potentially learning, and him helping to moderate. Only by mutual agreement, they had decided to skip the event and take advantage of the fact everyone else would hopefully be at it. The fact that Maria's was a local spot few tourists knew about— Brian had found it by chance the first year he'd attended the conference—added to the unlikelihood of being caught socializing together.

"Ready to admit I was right?" Brian asked from across the small, round table. A cocky grin curved his lips.

He was suggesting he'd been accurate about her sexual control freak tendencies being the problem with them, and that once she'd left her dominating ways behind, they had no problem. And the answer was no, because she wasn't buying it for a second.

Yeah, they'd had incredible sex. Yeah, she'd never come so hard before when she wasn't the one on top and making sure special attention was paid to all the right places. But, no, that did not have anything to do with her personality.

That he thought it did had Taryn rethinking that whole nice guy title she'd bestowed on him less than two hours ago. "I'm not a control freak. Yes, slowing things down a bit made everything that much better, but they can be almost as good fast. Just not with you."

Hurt passed through his eyes and then was gone quickly. He shrugged. "Hey, whatever you have to believe. The important thing is I'll always know the truth."

And she would always know she'd managed to upset him by mentioning other men.

Was it that she'd implied other men could make her feel almost as good going fast, or just that she'd mentioned other men altogether? If it were the first, it was a lie meant to save face. If it was the second, they needed to have a serious talk.

Which reminded her how little she still knew about him. At least, factual information. Now the question was where to start. With his business dealings, his mother's death, his ex-girlfriend he'd more or less denied having.

Reclining her elbows on the table, Taryn leaned forward and settled on the man himself. "Tell me about you. Real stuff I can't read in a tabloid."

"What? You don't believe I'm a heartless corporate shark anymore?"

"Maybe. Maybe—"

"Not," Brian finished for her. "I get your evasion technique, Taryn." Reaching across the table, he cupped her chin, then leaned forward and kissed her. A soft, tender kiss that left Taryn longing for so very much more.

He reclined in his chair and locked his fingers loosely over his middle. "Trust me, the gossip's much more exciting than the truth. I work ten- to twelve-hour or longer days, often seven days a week. Then to reward myself for good behavior, I take a vacation once a year to come here, and well, work more."

Honestly, the gossip on him hadn't been all that exciting sounding, but, yeah, he was right, it still sounded better than this. "So you never partake in pleasure?"

He straightened in his chair. "Is this about Serena?"

It hadn't been, though eventually she'd planned to lead up to the woman. Not that she actually cared if Serena had been Brian's girlfriend at some point in time—really, she didn't—she was just curious what it was about the woman that made her worthy of him sharing information on his mother. "Not unless you want to talk about her."

He visibly tensed. She presumed that meant he would be changing the subject; instead he said, "She wasn't exactly a girlfriend, but I guess as close to one as I've ever had. That was long ago, before I knew what I wanted in a woman."

Okay, so maybe the only reason he'd shared information on his mother with Serena was because she'd been handy, and he had yet to discover she wasn't the kind of woman to tell your secrets to. Not that Taryn actually knew anything about Serena. But if she wasn't good enough for Brian, she just plain wasn't good enough.

Taryn acknowledged that she was being irrational again, and forced herself to quit with the analyzing. There was no point when he was in a sharing mood. Apparently sex really did make some guys more open. "What is it you want in a woman?"

Another unidentifiable emotion passed through his eyes. This time when it slipped away, he reclined back in the chair, and, though he was looking directly at her, his focus seemed to be a million miles away. "Someone strong, not afraid to voice their opinion. Someone who isn't afraid to stand up against opposition or keep going when the odds seem against them. Someone will a real goal in their life. One that means more to them than money or power."

"Someone like me," Taryn interjected.

Brian's focus cleared, homed in on her so intensely her words struck home and she choked. What a completely moronic thing to say! "I mean...those characteristics sound like me, not that I'm right for you. I'm not. I mean, jeez, I live halfway across the freaking country. Besides, we don't even like each other. Not really."

"You don't like me?"

Nice. Now she'd done it, moved her big fat mouth right from the frying pan to the fire. He didn't look exactly upset by the comment, but then he wasn't smiling, either. But what was she supposed to have said? She had to make it clear she didn't think their relationship was headed somewhere serious. "Well, no. I mean not in the way that—"

"Brian?" A male voice cut her off. An instant later, a gray-haired guy who looked like he would have fit with the geriatric bunch on the nude beach came up to their table. "I thought that was you," the man said while Taryn attempted to flush completely unhealthy visions of old, naked people playing volleyball from her mind. *Eeuw!*

"Dayton Fox." Brian stood and reached out a hand. The older guy pushed it aside and enveloped him in a hug. He released Brian after a few seconds to glance at Taryn with a wide smile that showed he still had all his teeth. Either that, or really good dentures. "Good to see you looking so happy. Honeymooning?"

"Not even close," Brian responded without looking at her. "Taryn is... She's a songwriter attending the conference on the other side of the island. We happened to cross paths in the hotel lobby, both looking for an evening snack, so I suggested we come here. Is Muriel with you?"

"Up ordering." The old guy nodded toward the counter where a woman with unnaturally bright red hair and a matching sundress spoke with a café employee. He glanced back at them only to have Muriel call his name in a loud, shrill voice.

"I'd best head over before she starts making a scene to get my attention. It's great seeing you again," Dayton told Brian, then to Taryn, "A real pleasure meeting you." He looked back at Brian. "Stop by our table before you leave. After all that you've done for us, you know how much Muriel adores you. She'll be furious if she doesn't get to say hello."

"Thanks. We will."

As Dayton made his way toward his wife, Brian told Taryn he would go check on their food. A few minutes later, he returned with a tray carrying his double-bean burrito and her smothered nachos. After the way she'd been downing ice cream this week, and how little thought she'd given to exercise, she shouldn't eat them, but then you only lived once. Or, as Laurel had a habit of saying, twice if you're lucky.

Speaking of the Wiccan, Taryn should be in her hotel room, checking in with Sarah to see how last-minute details were progressing with the Wiccan Emporium's grand opening promotional plan. Only as she took her first bite of nachos and moaned and groaned over layer after layer of chips, beans, veggies, and stringy orange cheese, she knew she didn't want to be upstairs. She wanted to be here with Brian, getting to the bottom of who he was once and for all.

The way Dayton had acted as though he owed Brian his firstborn—or in the old guy's case, first grandchild—he obviously was a nice guy at least part of the time. She looked at Brian to see if his expression might give something about his relationship with the man away. The vacant look in his eyes wasn't saying anything.

Trying for levity, she asked, "So, you don't honestly think I would let that hug and the way

Dayton all but drooled over you pass without question, right?"

Brian looked up at her, his eyes no longer vacant, but unbearably cool. "I don't know. Do two people who aren't friends, just sleeping together, have a reason to share things like that?"

Ouch. Someone was a little upset.

"I didn't mean it like that. I just mean that... We live a long way apart, Brian. I appreciate your helping me out with my lyrics and everything, but when this week's over we're going home, back to reality. I can't ever come back to the conference. So, yes, we're friends, but only for another few days."

His hard look relented slightly. "I worked with him once."

"Not too long ago given how well he remembers you," Taryn said as warmly as possible, hoping to bring a complete thaw over him. "Muriel too, by the sounds of things. So, what did you do for him?"

Focusing on his plate, he stabbed a bite of burrito so fiercely she couldn't help but wonder if he would have preferred it be her neck. "His company was struggling. I gave him some pointers. That's all."

"Instead of buying it out and reselling to someone with a bigger pocketbook? Interesting." Argh! She should really learn to shut up. She already had him angry; now she was risking him turning that fork on her for real.

"I told you not to believe everything you read," Brian said, without looking up.

"Give me some idea of who the real man is, and I won't have to base my opinions on gossip."

Now he looked at her, and his gaze couldn't have been any more scathing. "We're temporary friends, Taryn. You just said yourself that this relationship isn't going to last beyond Sunday. Why do you care who I really am?"

* * *

He should have said good-bye to Taryn in the hotel lobby. Instead, Brian hadn't said anything at all from nearly the moment he'd brought their food back to the table at Maria's. Taryn hadn't said any more, either, though he could tell she wanted to. Likely would say something if he allowed her to stay in his room a second longer.

That had to be why she'd followed him to the room to begin with. She'd still lagged behind a bit, and then did the duck and run routine to his door, but she was here, sitting at his table, looking at him without saying a word.

"Speak," he ordered, not about to spend the rest of the night in this god-awful silence.

Fuck, it was hard to believe a little over an hour ago he'd been planning to spend it with her shapely legs and even shapelier body wrapped around him, riding him to the stars.

"I don't know what to say," Taryn admitted.

"Well, that's different. You speechless." The only other times she'd been at a loss for words was when he had his tongue stuck down her throat or making it known he planned to get it there soon. "Why did you come up to my room if you're just going to sit there and mope?"

That registered a flare of heat in her eyes, followed by a snapped, "I'm not moping."

"You are moping, and all because I repeated your own damned words."

The heat left her eyes. She sighed. "Look, I'm sorry. Okay? I didn't mean to hurt your feelings, or whatever. I figured you'd be glad to know I wasn't in this for the long haul. That I don't need any more huggy, lovey friends in my life. I already have plenty."

Yeah, well, he'd thought that way as well.

All that talk about his ideal woman had been something from his past. Since his mother's death, he'd made it a point to not stay with any one woman too long. If things started to get personal, he ended the relationship. He'd come to value his solitude. No attachments of any kind meant not needing to worry about something bad happening and someone being hurt for it.

So, yeah, he should have been glad Taryn spelled out what they were. But, damn it to hell, he wasn't. He wasn't, because aggressive and stubborn and, even, goofy as she could be at times, she'd been right when she'd said his ideal woman sounded like her.

She *was* his ideal woman. The type he purposefully avoided.

Brian had told himself he stayed away from her type because he dealt with dominant people too much through his business dealings, but deep down he always knew it was a lie. He avoided her type because they were the kind he respected the most, the kind who could really get to him. The kind he could see himself with in the long run. Only it wasn't just a type anymore; it was one woman. It was Taryn.

Son of a bitch!

Pushing a hand through his hair, when he would have preferred to pound it into the nearest wall, he crossed to the bed and sat down on the edge. The blinking light on the phone caught his attention. He picked up the receiver and pushed in the button for voice mail.

Probably someone calling to chew his ass out for missing tonight's event. He hadn't needed to be there, but he should have at least let someone know he wasn't attending. At the time all he'd been able to think about was Taryn and the sexual high she had him on.

He grunted into the receiver as the message started to play. Donald Shewson's gravelly voice came over the line. Brian spoke with the conference chair in passing, but it was odd that he would call.

Or not so odd, he realized as the message played on.

The tension radiating through him turned to that of another kind. His gut knotted with anxiety when Donald mentioned Taryn's name. That knotting turned to a painful burning sensation when the man ended the message by stating rather bluntly that he knew what the two of them were up to and that they needed to talk immediately.

"What's the matter?" Taryn asked, her voice ringing with concern. "You look...ill."

Not half as ill as she was about to look.

Brian chanced looking at her to deliver the news. "Maybe nothing, but...I think someone might have seen us together, doing something other than talking about the conference."

Chapter Sixteen

If Brian didn't get his ass back to this room in the next minute, Taryn would implode. Either that, or her bellyache would become so painful she would pass out. Maybe she would fall down and crack her head open because of him yet.

He'd gone to track down Donald Shewson over an hour ago. If he hadn't been able to find him, Brian would have come right back. That he hadn't returned meant he had found Donald, and right now they were talking about throwing Taryn out of the conference for a few minutes of bad sex with a total prick.

All right, so the sex they'd had today was the polar opposite of bad. And it had lasted well beyond a few minutes. Honestly, she couldn't even call Brian a total prick anymore. But he still wasn't a nice guy. Nope. He was just plain *B-A-D*.

The click of the key card outside the door had Taryn springing to her feet from the chair she'd been sitting in like a zombie since Brian left. Seconds later, the door opened and he walked through it. The look on his face could only be described as...

Hell, Taryn didn't know what, but he didn't look happy.

Her belly twisted like an out-of-control roller coaster. The blood thundered between her temples. She could all but see hope floating away. "So I'm screwed? Tossed out of the conference. Might as well pack my bags and kiss my sorry ass good-bye right now, huh?"

He came toward her, arms out, like he was going to pull her into a comforting hug. "I tried to point out that I'm not judging this year. That I—"

"Hey, I knew the rules from the start." Taryn sidestepped his touch. Heartbreak turned to anger as she realized how inaccurate those words were. "Wait, no I didn't. *You* knew the rules from the start. *I* didn't learn them until after Willy had made his encore performance."

Brian winced, and his voice came out nearly as short as hers had. "Guess that means we're back to everything bad in your life being my fault."

"This *is* your fault! If you hadn't been such a lousy lay five years ago, I would never have spent all that time thinking about you, hating you, wishing to God you'd stay out of my head. I sure as hell wouldn't have felt the need to give you another try, let alone three more.

"I can't believe I fell for your crap. Acting like you actually cared about my music, like you didn't just say that to get me back in bed, so you could heal your poor pathetic ego. I thought you actually wanted to help me out." She snorted. "Well, you know what? You did, Brian, you helped me out. Right out of my dream."

"I do care about your music, and I did want to help you. But you don't need my help. You don't need anyone's help. You just need to believe in yourself and not be afraid to let that belief come through in your lyrics. You're good, Taryn. You'll go places, with or without this conference."

So now he thought that her music was dandy, it was her that had the problem. Just one of many things wrong with her in his eyes. To think she'd nearly had herself convinced that he was a nice guy. Yeah, right, and inhaling pint after pint of Chocolate Cashew Heaven was good for her waistline.

Fat chance!

"Whatever," Taryn retorted. Pressure at the backs of her eyes and building in her throat suggested heartbreak was attempting to overtake anger again. Not about to stand here and let him witness her breaking down, she moved to the door. "I don't need this," she said, opening it and hurrying through.

If Brian replied, the words were cut off by the slamming of the door and the mad gush of tears that filled her eyes as she rushed for the elevator.

* * *

He hated apologizing. Was rotten at it.

Most of all, Brian couldn't think of a single reason why he should be the one doing the apologizing. It had to be because one part of Taryn's accusation was right on. He had known about the "no relations with the conference staff" rule from day one. Those first couple of days, before the conference began, he hadn't given it much thought. After that...after that Taryn had known about it, as well, and had voluntarily come to him.

Damn it, this was not his fault.

The only reason he was doing the dirty work and going to her room to apologize was because he didn't want her leaving the island hating him. The flight that would take her home wouldn't arrive on Sugar Foot until Sunday, but if Taryn was as mad—or rather, as hurt—today as she had been last night, he could see her taking another flight, somewhere completely out of her way, just to get away from him and the conference as a whole.

She couldn't leave, because they had some serious talking to do. Particularly after what she said about not being able to get him out of her head for the last five years. The truth was that she had been in the back of his all that time too. Not as a constant thought, but one that returned every couple of months and made him wonder what had happened to her.

Thoughts of Taryn had been with him much more frequently, in truth, on a daily basis, during those last few weeks of his mother's life. At the time, Brian had no idea why. Now he knew. Now he accepted the reason, just as he'd accepted that she was his ideal woman. Quite simply because Taryn reminded him of the one person he'd respected the most—his mom.

Not physically, of course, but in her external strength, her determination, her lack of supporters, and the drive to excel even without that encouragement. Taryn claimed to have many people who believed in her, loved her. Her too often exposed insecurities said otherwise.

Yeah, they had a lot of talking to do. That meant he needed to get this truce thing right the first time.

Brian reached Taryn's room and shifted the ice cream he'd picked up as a make-up gift from his right hand to his left. He considered knocking hard and calling out, "Open up!" the way she always did to him, but then opted not to, since that was liable to be all it would take to make her not answer the door. He settled on a quick rap, then stepped out of view of the peephole.

The door opened a few seconds later, and he returned to the spot in front of it. Taryn stood there, her silky black hair floating riotously around her face, her sexy curves decked out in little gray cotton shorts and a pink, breast-hugging tank top that, even now, had a direct effect on his dick. Her feet were bare, and her toenails painted a siren red that made his mouth water.

He hadn't gotten around to exploring her feet. Would they be ticklish? Her toes a delicacy she squealed and squirmed over when he sucked on them?

His balls snugged in interest, and he bit back the image forming with a grunt. Was it possible that they'd just had sex yesterday? Twice?

Her face went from moderately tranquil to infuriated, assuring Brian they had in fact had sex twice yesterday and that it was the very reason they weren't speaking. Just in case that wasn't clear enough for him, she followed the look up with, "Leave me alone!"

Taryn started to slam the door. He stuck his foot in its path before she could close it all the way. "We need to talk." When her annoyed look didn't fade, he lifted the pint in his arm. "I brought you a present."

Her attention wavered to the ice cream. For an instant, he saw the joyful effect it had on her, and then she shook her head. "Ice cream is not going to make this better, you idiot!"

So he was going to have to pull out all the stops and actually say the words. He could handle that. He was a big boy. "Would hearing how sorry I am help? Because I swear to you, Taryn, I am—"

"Nothing will help. I don't want to talk to you, Brian." She blinked at him several times, before saying in a quiet, shaky voice, "Just go. Please. I really want to be alone."

Brian hadn't planned to leave for anything—he'd planned to stand at this door and make a complete fool of himself it that was what it took to earn her forgiveness—but the tears that welled in her eyes changed his mind.

He could guess at how brokenhearted she was over losing her chance to share her music in the conference showcase when many of the industry bigwigs would be in attendance. The anguish on her face last night suggested she'd already spent a good deal of tears over the situation. He wouldn't make her cry any more. If she needed distance from him to stop that from happening, he would give it to her. For a few hours.

He pulled his foot from the door. Without a word, Taryn closed it the rest of the way. Before he could move, the door opened back up and her hand shot out and grabbed the pint of ice cream.

She squeaked out a, "Thanks," and shut the door again.

Brian stared at the door for a few seconds, and then his heavy thoughts turned to appeased ones. He grinned as he started down the hallway. Taryn might have said ice cream wouldn't fix things—and he knew she was right as far as the conference went—but so long as she was accepting gifts from him, he hoped it was a start toward fixing things between them.

* * *

She was acting like a bitch.

Taryn knew it, and that Brian was no more at fault for what happened than she was. She'd rolled the dice, run with the idea that if he wasn't a real judge, then there was the potential it wouldn't matter if she slept with him again. In the end, it hadn't just been judges the conference attendees were to keep their distance from, but anyone who held influence in the decision-making process on the whole.

She should have sought clarification on that point. Not that it would have mattered. Because even as she screamed at him last night like a total nutcase, she'd longed for his arms. Even as she'd bawled like a baby the better part of the night, she'd wanted him in her bed. Even as she ordered him away from her room today, she'd ached for him. Just opening the door to see him standing there had her blood firing with carnal need, her pussy quaking for his touch.

She'd tried to drown her misery in ice cream. Not even that worked. All she wanted was Brian. To come back to her room and tell her how good her music was, how much he believed in her. To give her another lesson in how completely gratifying playing the part of the submissive and letting go of control could feel. She wanted his magical hands all over her, soothing with soft caresses, dampening with brazen strokes. Those sexy, sensual lips moving against hers, pressing along the curve of her neck, nibbling on her ear.

If he was here right now, she would—

A knock sounded on the door. A knock that sounded exactly like the soft yet serious one Brian used twenty minutes ago. Hope sailed through her to the point of apprehension. Trying to regain some of her earlier anger, Taryn lodged the pint of ice cream in the crook of her arm and stood from the bed. With a snarl in place, she went to the door and tossed it open, not bothering to look through the peephole. The sight of Sarah brought twin forces of disappointment and relief.

"What are you doing here?" Taryn asked.

"Laurel said you needed me"—Sarah cast her gaze the length of her, her nose curling—"and by the looks of things she was right. Have you even brushed your hair today? And what is that in your arm?" Apparently the question was rhetorical, as Sarah gave her head a sad shake, sending her long blonde tresses into action. "It's even worse than Laurel thought. Dare I ask how many pints have come before that one?"

Two. But neither had been eaten to make her feel better. Both were surprisingly thoughtful gifts from Brian.

Sighing, Taryn focused on her friend's unplanned arrival. "What about work?" she asked when Sarah dropped her travel bag and settled on the love seat. "What about Laurel's grand opening? How could you leave all that behind after we agreed how important it was that one of us be there this week? It's the reason I had to come here alone, remember?"

"Chill out, Tare. The business can survive being closed one Friday out of the year. And Laurel's grand opening isn't until next week. Besides, I told you she's the one who said I needed to come here. She said your negative energy's so high you're liable to combust." Sarah frowned. "I can totally see she was right. You look megafrazzled. Is it because of Brian? Did you have more bad sex with him? Honey, he didn't hurt you, did he? Make you fall for him a second time only to break your heart all over again?"

Taryn almost dropped the ice cream. Despite what she led Sarah to believe, she hadn't fallen for Brian five years ago. And she for sure hadn't, or wasn't in the process of, doing so now. He was sort of an okay guy, but they weren't even friends beyond the short-term. Given how Brian had behaved in regard to their temporary friendship, if anyone was falling here, it was him.

Her heart skipped a beat. No way! Could it be possible he really had fallen for her?

He'd made it clear she and her supposedly aggressive personality weren't his usual type. But if that was true, if he went for the more submissive female, then it didn't gel with the way he'd described his ideal woman. He'd made her out to be strong, independent—not afraid to take on a challenge even when the odds were against her. As Taryn said at the time, he'd made his ideal woman sound like her.

"Come back to the world of the living and talk to me, Tare. I didn't spend the last eight hours hopping from one plane to the next to talk to a zombie."

Her friend showing up was a huge surprise, but quite possibly a benefit. If there was even a chance Brian was falling for her, or, God forbid, had already fallen, then keeping her distance was imperative. She had made dinner and dancing plans with Dawn earlier in the week for this evening. Taryn had decided to break them after what happened—she'd considered skipping the island altogether, on the first plane or boat out—but now she realized keeping the plans was critical.

As was getting the topic off Brian. "The sex was great." Okay, so that wasn't the best way to make her stop thinking about him. "But he's nowhere close to my heart. He just got me thrown out of the conference, that's all."

Sarah's eyes went wide. "That's all?" she yelped. "Last time we talked you said your songwriting career depended on this conference. So unless you've changed your mind about that again, allow me to say, what a prick."

"I exaggerated. I was mad at him then, but now I...I was wrong. He's not a prick, Sarah." Taryn held out the ice cream. "He brought me this."

"Ice cream? He brought you ice cream to make up for being a total creep, and you forgave him?"

Sarah was getting this all wrong. Brian was not a total creep. He was a nice guy. He believed in her. Had helped her to find her passion so she could write a song she felt great about. She wouldn't get to sing that song during the showcase, but there would be other chances. If those chances took years to arrive, she had the promotional company and her commercial jingles to keep her going. She wasn't exactly a starving artist.

"This isn't his fault. At least, not all his fault. I knew the risks involved. He tried to get the judges to reconsider. I have to give him credit for that." She should give him an apology too, for the way she'd acted last night and again a short while ago, but that would mean seeing him again. While she now had nothing to fear in getting caught going to his room, it was still a definite no-no.

Taryn would walk into his room, he'd toss that sexy grin her way, and she would be toast. Vapor. A trembling little mass of nerves just waiting for him to touch her, kiss her, hold her. Stroke her, lick her. Take her.

Her pussy pulsed with wetness, and she sighed.

There would be no going to his room to apologize, or even going within twenty feet of him. It just wasn't safe. What was safe, and even better a good idea, was finally tracking down her island hottie.

She'd been right all along. This want she felt for Brian was nothing more than that: want, lust. She was horny, in need of another lay. Any guy would do.

"You like him, don't you?"

Taryn caught the hint of amusement in Sarah's voice and knew how loaded that question was. By "like" she meant a whole lot more than like. "Yes, I like him, as a friend, nothing more permanent, and my emotions are absolutely not involved. He's just a temporary friend I happened to have great sex with."

There she went reflecting on sex with Brian again. But her horny assessment was right on. He had been her first lay of the year, so, annually speaking, she had nothing to compare him with. Truth be told, the sex was probably mediocre at best, and, yeah, his little game of "play submissive for me" seemed like it made the main event last longer than ever before, but that was probably just a figment of her imagination.

"If you two are such great temporary pals, why aren't you with him now? You're already out of the conference, so why are you here gorging yourself and looking unkempt when you could be in his room huffing and puffing and playing Strip Pudding? And that's the second time you said the sex was great. Did you take my advice on giving him another chance to prove himself, or when did you stop using his name and speedy in the same sentence?"

"Last night. And I'm not with him because there are hundreds of other great-looking guys on this island waiting for an introduction to my little red wrapper." Which would probably be two sizes too small after all the ice cream she'd downed since last wearing it that first night when she had bad sex with Brian again.

And that was more than enough about Brian.

Taryn set the almost empty pint of ice cream on the sitting area table and smiled at her friend. Next week she would be home scraping ice off her windshield and shivering in the freezing cold. Tonight she was on a stunning tropical island about to meet lucky guy number two. "I'm going out tonight for dinner and dancing. Since you came all this way just to check out my negative energy, so are you."

Sarah stood and followed Taryn to the closet. "You're for real going to go to dinner and dancing with someone else, even though Brian is now great in bed and a good guy on top of that?"

"I am." Taryn concentrated on her wardrobe so she wouldn't be tempted to think about Brian yet again. "I'm supposed to meet my friend in the lobby in a half hour, so we both had better get moving."

"What does this friend look like? I mean for as hot as you make Brian out to be, this new guy must be babealicious and then some."

Yep, this concentrating thing was really working. She'd hardly even noticed that Sarah mentioned Brian's name and the word hot in the same sentence. "He's a she, and cute. You'll like her."

"Oh, good, maybe I'll give bi a try for lucky guy, make that gal, number seven."

Taryn's focus evaporated, and she swiveled around to gape at Sarah.

Her friend laughed as she squatted next to her travel bag and unzipped it. "Kidding. You know I'm always game for a girls' night out. And it just so happens I brought a little something along in the event I should decide to end my girls' night out by letting a guy come on in."

"Big surprise," Taryn said with a laugh of her own.

"Even bigger surprise, I brought something for you too." Sarah pulled a shimmering silver dress from the bag and handed it to her. "From what Laurel said, I guessed you'd need a pick-me-up, and if this dress won't find the guy to do that, nothing will."

"Wow. It's..." Even smaller than her favorite little red wrapper.

The belly and back were wide-open, with only a thin patch of flesh-colored mesh holding what little material made up the top and bottom halves of the strapless dress together.

"Tawdry. Slutty. Perfect for a hot, steamy island fling." Sarah shot her a conspiratorial wink. "I know. That's why I bought myself three of them in different colors. Trust me, hon, if lucky guys five and six knew what they were talking about, the dress works no matter what the temperature is outside."

Chapter Seventeen

She did not want to be here.

Taryn had considered throwing a tantrum over coming to the Strobe. The bar made her think of Brian—more notably, of dancing with Brian. Or maybe that should be having sex with Brian on the dance floor, with their clothes on, because they'd come damned close to doing just that.

Sarah had asked about the hot spot for dancing and manhunting at the front desk while Taryn sought out Dawn. By the time they'd regrouped, Sarah had the Strobe stuck in her head and soon convinced Dawn it was the place to be. Taryn gave in, and here she was, back in the land of blackness and shifting strobe lights that each time they moved, revealed another half-dressed couple, threesome, or more, gearing up for a fuck or already getting it on.

"This is...interesting," Dawn observed, as they waited for drinks.

"We could go somewhere else, if you'd rather." Taryn hoped the loud music veiled the "please say yes" quality of her voice. "I heard there was a—"

"No," Dawn said resolutely, her attention on the scene below. "I want to be here. When I was with Jeff I would never have thought about coming somewhere like this. I'm a different person now. I want to be wild."

"You go girl," Sarah chimed in loudly while scanning the crowd below. "That's the—No way! It cannot be him."

"Who?" Taryn asked.

"My butt guy is down there with some hoochie. You know the one we passed in the hallway of the Seaside, and I almost swallowed my tongue over? I cannot believe he's here. Or that a man can look so damned fine in all black."

Taryn scoped out the crowd until she spotted the man in question grinding against a woman on a small, elevated platform. "He looks somewhat familiar, but that's not him, Sarah."

"Who's *him*?" Dawn asked.

"She thinks that guy on the middle platform, dancing with the woman in the blue bodysuit, is Mike Carmichael, the conference judge who was involved in the day-two interview sessions."

Dawn squinted and, when the strobe lights returned to the couple in question, shook her head. "You're right. He does look a little familiar, but Mike has light brown hair and glasses. It's dark in here, but not dark enough to make light brown hair look black."

"That guy in the hotel had hair?" Sarah asked, her attention riveted on the dance floor. "Guess I was looking elsewhere." She made a picture frame with her thumbs and first fingers and centered the man's ass in it. Her whistle was just loud enough to hear above the din. "I'm telling you, that is the same guy. Maybe he's wearing a wig and contacts, or something, but I always remember my asses. Especially ones that look this fine."

Taryn laughed. Sarah did have a habit of remembering her butts, but this time she was wrong. Mike looked nowhere as good as this guy did as he moved blatantly against the hoochie, who incidentally might be wearing a tight bodysuit, but it was still more than either Sarah or Taryn had on. "Why don't you go cut in, or join them? The way this place is, I'm sure they won't mind."

Sarah looked back with a frown. "I don't like sharing."

"Please, like you'll have to share wearing that dress. He'll take one look at you and realize his current partner looks more ready for the senior prom."

Sarah's lips, painted deep burgundy to match her barely there dress, curved into a satiated smile. "Yeah, he will. Okay, wish me luck."

"Good luck." As if she would need it.

"Have fun," Dawn called to her already retreating back. "Hey, do you want us to get you a drink?"

"Don't bother wasting your breath," Taryn said. "She's in seek-and-destroy mode. Until she has him begging to go home with her, she won't be back."

Sarah found them ten minutes later sipping drinks near a far corner of the bar. If it weren't for the huge grin on her face, Taryn would have thought the impossible had happened and she'd been turned down.

Reaching them, Sarah sang out, "Same guy."

Impossible. That guy and Mike looked nothing alike. A wig, contacts, and a change of clothing could accomplish a lot, but no, it was too unbelievable. "Did you ask him, or why do you think that?"

"His eyes. They're incredibly dark, intense. Between that and his tight ass and his scent—sooo good—I can't be wrong."

"You said you didn't notice his hair earlier," Taryn pointed out. "How was it you managed to remember his eyes?"

"I did notice his hair, just not the exact color. And how could you not notice those eyes? Yeah, he had glasses on, but even then they were so vivid...mmm...it makes me wet just thinking about them." She gave a shiver and then glanced back in the direction she'd come from. "I told him I'd be right back, I just wanted to let my friends know they were looking like lame-os standing over here holding up the wall. Go fishing, girls, you both look hot!"

"Yes, Mom," Taryn said as Sarah made her way back through the crush of moving, thriving, thrusting bodies.

"I don't think that's Mike," Dawn spoke her thoughts.

"It's not, but let her have her little fantasy." They shared a laugh, and then Taryn said, "Actually, I do want to get some dancing in." Truthfully she wanted to get on the floor and find her island hottie. Dawn knew about what had happened with Brian—the whole conference probably did by now—and so while the blonde claimed to be ready to cut her wild side loose, Taryn figured she'd be better off not spelling out the fact she planned to go home with a stranger tonight.

She took a draining sip of her martini, stuffed the olive into her mouth, and then set the glass on the shelf built into the wall. "Ready, wild child?"

Dawn glanced at the dance floor and back at her half-full margarita. "One sec." She tipped the glass back, guzzled to the last drop, and slammed it down on the shelf. "Liquid courage in place. Ready to rumba."

More like do the Butthump Boogie, Taryn thought ten minutes later. She'd lost sight of Dawn in her attempt to escape the guy behind her, the one who was disgustingly aroused and making every effort to show her. He wasn't bad looking, just...not what she had in mind for her island hottie. His hair was black, and that was great, but his eyes were too dark to be green, and she really did love green eyes. And his face was clean-shaven, no stubble at all. And he hadn't even come close to nuzzling her neck or whispering in her ear.

So pretty much, he wasn't Brian.

Taryn blew out a breath and made herself respond to Butthump Boy's moves while she glanced over at Sarah. Unlike Dawn, Sarah and her man-who-was-not-Mike were in plain view. They still danced on the elevated platform, and each time the lights landed on them, everyone in the club could see what they were doing. Sarah's hands were either under the guy's shirt or stuck down the back of his pants. Knowing Sarah's ass-fetish, Taryn would guess down his pants.

Or not, Taryn realized a few seconds later when Sarah's hands emerged from under his shirt. Her fingers curled at the hem, slowly lifting the black silk up his back. Probably in an attempt to see his chest, Taryn thought absently, and then forgot all about that thought as a distinct image took shape on the man's back.

Taryn's legs stopped moving, her hips ceased swaying. She wasn't even aware of Butthump Boy behind her anymore. All she could see was Sarah's man. Sarah's man with his big, black, ugly snake on his back.

Snake Guy!

The pulse of a wild island beat and strobe lights casting through blackness and a sea of moving bodies came back to Taryn in a jarring blur. Heart hammering, she broke away from Butthump Boy and darted through the crowd to the platform. With a tug on Sarah's elbow, she jerked her from Snake Guy's arms.

Sarah swung around, eyes narrowed, and mouthed, *What?*

Emergency, Taryn mouthed back.

Better be good, Sarah returned. She gave Snake Guy a kiss that made Taryn's belly curl and then followed her to the quietest part of the bar, before shouting, "What is so important? I was just about to close the deal."

Close the deal. In other words go home with that sleaze, or bring him back to their hotel room. Yuck! "That is not Mike. It's Snake Guy!"

Sarah huffed. "It is Mike. He told me so himself. Now if you're done being a total spaz—"

"That *is* Mike?" He'd actually admitted to Sarah who he was? Or maybe Sarah had suggested her friend had called him Mike, and he'd merely agreed with her. "Did he recognize me?"

Sarah's disgruntled look caved slightly. "Yeah, he knows who you are. He said to tell you he was sorry to hear about your getting booted from the conference."

Then he really was Mike. Mike was Snake Guy. Mike was a sleazeball. Taryn grabbed hold of Sarah's arm. Sarah could hate her all she wanted; there was no way she was letting her go back to him. "You don't want him, Sarah. He might seem nice, but he's not. He's been with a different woman every day since we've been here. I saw him, literally."

Her eyes widened. "You saw him having sex? Like, saw him saw him?"

"Yes." And at the time she'd been turned on by it. Turned on and wishing Brian was with her, so that they could partake in some dirty beach fun too. "It was a mistake, but I saw him, and then the next day I saw him with another woman. They were kissing and laughing like they'd been together for some time and...and you deserve someone better. Like...like...like a cowboy," Taryn finished on a rush when she spotted a familiar white Stetson.

Who would ever have thought she'd be so glad to see the cocky cowboy who'd shared her dinner table that first night? She flagged him over with a yell and then a wild gesture, aware she looked like a lunatic, but then desperate times called for desperate measures.

"Ladies." He knocked a finger against the brim of his hat and flashed a gap-toothed smile. "How goes it? Taryn, right?"

"Yes." She flashed a brilliant smile Sarah's way. "This is my friend Sarah, who's looking for someone to dance with."

Cowboy's smile went from cordial to a full-out grin that brought forth a dimple, which made him look decidedly attractive in a boy-next-door sort of way. The grin fell when Sarah jerked her arm from Taryn's grasp, and snapped, "I am not. I am having a great time with Mike. Now if you don't mind..."

"Saw you two up there," Cowboy said, stopping Sarah from storming off. "Don't know if you're here for the conference or not, but I reckon you might wanna be careful with that one. Heard he isn't afraid to take a physical bribe to help sway his judging decision."

Taryn's attempts to stop Sarah ground to a halt. She gasped, "You think women are sleeping with him in order to do better?"

Cowboy shrugged. "Might just be rumors. Haven't seen nothing myself."

Had she? Were those women she'd seen Mike with this week from the conference? Whether they were or not, one thing was clear, Mike was a first-class slime. She turned imploring eyes on Sarah. "If you are truly my best friend and love me, you'll promise not to sleep with him."

Sarah's expression was unreadable as she asked Cowboy, "You for real think this guy's taking advantage of the conference to get laid?"

"Like I said, I haven't seen nothing, but there's a good chance."

Sarah nodded. Her lips curved into a smile Taryn had seen more than enough to fear. It was her naughty smile, the one she got when she was about to say or do something slightly immoral in the name of revenge. "What?" Taryn asked. "Why do you have that look on your face?"

"Think about it, Tare. Laurel said you needed me here. This is why, to catch this creep. There is no way that they can kick you out of the conference and let the women this guy's slept with stay in. I'll find out who they are and threaten to expose him and all of them, unless he sees to it that you're let back in."

Yep, just as she'd feared, a slightly immoral plan, concocted more or less in the name of revenge. Worse than learning her fear was right on, was that Taryn's belly lurched with hope.

She shouldn't even think about letting Sarah attempt to unveil Mike's unprofessional behavior. What she should be doing is following through on the plan herself. Only Taryn's reputation preceded her, from what had happened with Brian. There was no way Mike would take the bait if she tried to plant it.

Damn it, she should not be considering this. But she was. A lot. "How would you do it? What makes you think he even has that much authority?"

Sarah's eyes twinkled while her grin went from naughty to all-out wicked. "He might not right now, honey, but with the right ultimatum, you'd be surprised what a person can accomplish."

Chapter Eighteen

She wasn't going to his room for sex. She was *not* going to his room for sex.

This was not about wanting Brian so badly that Taryn had compared every guy she'd danced with tonight to him. She was simply going to his room at one thirty in the morning, wearing a dress that barely covered her crotch, to apologize.

Earlier her only thought had been to avoid him. Now she knew she had to deal with him. First, because the reason he'd been in her head all night was because she felt guilty over the way she treated him. And second, because she had more than enough to lie awake, thinking about tonight. Mainly, if Sarah would return safely and soon.

Sarah had left the Strobe with Snake Guy—Mike—shortly after midnight. Taryn's guilt had gotten the better of her, and she'd tried to convince her friend not to go, that exposing the sleazeball wasn't worth her spending time alone with him. But Sarah had her mind made up, and when that happened, there was no changing it. She'd assured Taryn she had her cell phone and that if anything even a little bad happened, she would call immediately. Then Sarah had tacked on if she couldn't reach Taryn at her room, she'd try Brian's.

Taryn snorted at the ridiculousness of the words as she stepped off the elevator onto the eighth floor. She would not be spending the night with Brian any more than she would be having sex with him.

She glanced around out of instinct as she made her way down the dimmed, deserted hallway. There was no longer a reason to sneak around. Even if there was, most people were probably asleep. Much like Brian.

Hoping she was wrong, Taryn knocked softly, then a bit louder. Twenty seconds passed, and the door remained closed, the room silent. Obviously, he *was* sleeping, and she should go back to her room and try to do the same.

Unless he wasn't asleep. Unless he just hadn't heard her. After all, she generally yelled for him.

With a quick look around, she pounded the door three times hard and said in a voice just shy of a shout, "Brian, are you awake?"

Another twenty seconds passed, then thirty, then a full minute. It was clear he wasn't awake, or maybe he wasn't even home. Maybe he had plans tonight. With another woman.

Taryn's belly did a slow roll. She'd gone out looking for another man tonight with the express purpose of getting laid. She had no right to feel upset if Brian had chosen to do the same. Really, it didn't matter if he had. It wasn't like she cared about him or anything. They were barely friends. As she'd told Sarah, her emotions were not involved, even a little bit.

The rustle of a chain lock sounded. The door made a snicking noise, then opened to reveal Brian dressed in black, loose-fitting shorts and nothing else. Taryn lost all track of time and place. All thought but that of his delicious chest on full display. Inches from her lips, her tongue.

If she leaned forward even the slightest bit, they'd be touching. Tasting.

Her blood warmed. Her gaze slid south. The front of his shorts gained a noticeable tilt. A whimper escaped her, and that tilt grew. Just a little more and she wouldn't even need to lean. A simple nudge and his cock would be rubbing against her belly. A tiny step and his chest would be teasing across her breasts.

Wetness pooled in her panties. *Mmm mmm good.*

"I would've answered sooner," he explained, "but I just got into bed when I heard you knocking and had to throw something on. What's the matter?"

Too many things to count. Starting with how elated she was to find him here instead of out doing some other woman, and ending with the mere sight of his chest and the implication he slept nude was all it took to seriously arouse her.

With what felt like Herculean effort, Taryn met his eyes. "I was hoping to talk to you. It can wait until morning, though."

Brian stepped back from the doorway. "Come in. I'm not that tired."

Yeah, neither was she, and therein lay the problem.

Breezing past him, she stopped outside the bathroom. It was impossible to have sexual thoughts when standing so close to a toilet, right? "What I have to say will only take a second."

He closed the door, and joined her near the bathroom. Too near. He was invading her personal space in a big way.

"I stopped by your room a couple of times earlier," he said.

"I was out. At the Strobe."

His eyes went dark, predatory, primal. His gaze drifted from her face to her neck to her breasts and downward. Lingering on her bare belly had her pussy clenching uncontrollably and the rest of her fighting the urge to squirm.

"How is it you managed to come home alone looking like that?"

Taryn's nipples beaded with the sensual roughness of his voice. "I wasn't there looking for a man," she lied.

Brian's gaze relented its caress of her belly only to restart the sensual torment on her breasts. His lips parted a fraction, enough to peek out his tongue, remind her how wickedly good it felt teasing damp circles across her breasts. Her thoughts swam with her restless ache. Her nipples visibly stabbed against the dress. Swallowing on a hard breath, she reached for them. Thumbed the erect buds through the thin material in an attempt to relieve the pressure.

A slow, sexy grin slid over his lips. "You sure?"

Sure of what? She couldn't think for a nanosecond, let alone remember, when he was looking at her that way, like he wanted to eat her alive.

The vision of Brian on his knees, head between her bare thighs, lips and tongue feasting on her swollen cunt swirled through her head. Her sex stabbed with erotic heat. The breath snagged in her throat.

Taryn shook her head. *Concentrate. Remember why you're here. Standing feet away from a toilet, for cripes sake!*

Stuffing her hands at her sides, she said in a rush, "I came to apologize for treating you so badly last night. My getting booted from the conference sucks, but it wasn't your fault any more than my own."

"No. It wasn't," he agreed, that damn sexy rough quality of his voice still intact. "But you were right about my knowing about the 'no relations' rule before you did. I hadn't even considered it that night we were at the Strobe. Blame it on that scrap of red you called a dress, but the second I saw you in that thing, my brain bolted to my dick."

Her gaze darted to his shorts of its own accord. The bob of his cock against the thin cotton had her attention rushing back to his eyes in search of safer territory. Only the reckless hunger there was not safe. Not even slightly.

"Little as that thing was, I'd say you managed to top it tonight. You look hot as hell." Brian's hand shot out. His thumb found her belly and stroked. "Did you pick this out because of the open stomach?"

Her spinning thoughts turned to mush with the simple contact. She watched his fingers in a slow, sensual daze. "Huh?"

"If what you said during the icebreaker session held any truth, then you like to have your navel licked. I could get my tongue on it just by dropping to my knees."

Concentrate. Freaking concentrate!

Taryn drew her gaze back on his face. She forced herself not to tremble, not to so much as sigh, and only stammered slightly when she said, "Um. Y-yeah. So, anyway, I just wanted to say I'm sorry about acting so rude. I was ticked off, but I shouldn't have taken it out on you. You said you tried to talk to Donald about keeping me on, and I believe you."

"I did. I tried to make him understand how great your writing is, how determined you are to make it." His grin took on a salacious note, much like Sarah's did right before she did something naughty.

"I did leave a few things out," Brian continued, the thickness of his voice and the carnal invitation in his eyes a sure sign that he in fact planned to be naughty, and, oh damn, was she strong enough to resist? "Like your biggest dream about becoming a songwriter. How you want to be lying naked in bed and hear your song come on the radio right at that moment when your lover is taking your nipple between his lips, running his hands down your hot, sweaty body. Then moving his mouth lower, along your ribs, deep into your navel to lick. Suck. Taste your sexy scent." Her breath caught audibly, and he added, "I also didn't tell him how much you love a challenge."

Is that what this was, a challenge? A test to see if he could goad her into sleeping with him again? He couldn't. She was almost sure of it.

Taryn crossed her arms and forced a chill into her voice, while the rest of her sizzled to the boiling point. "What are you doing, Brian?"

"I came to your room this afternoon to apologize. I felt damned bad about what happened. I still do. I don't want it to come between us. Fine if all you want is temporary friendship, but why can't it last until Sunday? Why do we have to deny ourselves what it's clear we're both aching for?"

"I'm not aching for you." No, her nipples always felt this stiff and throbbed so fiercely, it was a wonder she couldn't hear them. Her pussy was consistently wet to the extent she could give the Atlantic a run for its money.

"I am for you. My cock's so hard I might live up to that Speedy nickname yet and come in my shorts." He glanced down at his tented shorts. "Feel me."

"No!"

He laughed. "Scared?"

Terrified. Not of him, but of her weakness where he was concerned. She had always been able to say no to sex before, but now, now she didn't think she could. Didn't think she wanted to. But she had to. Because saying yes could lead to consequences. "I don't get scared."

"Maybe not about sex, but you do about your songwriting. Don't second-guess yourself just because not everyone believes in you. You're too good for that. Too strong. Too sexy."

"What does sexy have to do with my songwriting?" And why did he have to go and pull out the big guns? Wasn't it enough she wanted to cave to him when he was just talking about sex? Did he have to remind her yet again how much he believed in her?

"Probably not much," Brian admitted with a throaty chuckle. His thumb resumed its slow, torturous rub over her belly. "My brain isn't functioning on all cylinders, hasn't been since I opened the door to see you wearing damned near nothing.

"I want to see you wearing nothing, Taryn. You know that's what you want too."

"I see myself wearing nothing all the time."

"Not with me you don't. We both know you can't back down from a challenge. So how's this one for you?"

His finger left her belly, and in the next instant he stripped his shorts down his legs. The solid length of his cock jutted out at her, teasing, tempting. Precum pearled on the thick pink head. Her tongue went wild. Her fingers itched to savor.

Turning, he moved into the bathroom, flashed that delectably tight ass her way. And then, as if she needed any more persuasion, he threw down the gauntlet. "I'll be in the bathroom if you want me, living out my Jacuzzi fantasy."

Chapter Nineteen

"There's a very good chance that I hate you."

Brian chuckled at the bite in Taryn's voice, a bite that had nothing on the sizzling hunger darkening her eyes to that arresting shade of midnight. "I think you like me." He stood from the ledge built into the side of the Jacuzzi and glanced at his rock-solid dick. "I'd say it's clear that I like you."

She batted her eyelashes as a coy smile flirted with her lips. "Wow. All for little ol' me?"

"No one else."

The playfulness left her expression. She moved to the edge of the Jacuzzi. "I told myself I wouldn't do this when I came here."

"Why?" And why had she gone from teasing to serious?

"I know what a softy you are, how easily you fall for a girl. I don't want you getting too used to me, only to be heartbroken when I leave in a couple days."

The teasing had moved back into her voice. As such, Brian responded with a laugh, but even to him the sound wasn't quite authentic. He wouldn't be heartbroken when she left, but he would miss her, and the way she messed with his head one moment and sought out his help the next. He would regret knowing he let his ideal woman slip through his fingers. But the more he'd thought about it today, the more it had become obvious things couldn't last, not when they lived hundreds of miles apart and not when neither was willing to open up.

In a couple of days, Taryn would be gone. Now she was here.

Mine for the taking.

He grinned with the pleasure in that thought. "Here I thought you had a problem with insecurity."

The narrowing of her eyes told him the accusation hit home. Before she could voice a word of denial, he leaned over the Jacuzzi's edge, grabbed her around the waist, and pulled her into the water, killer black fuck-me heels and all. Wrenching out of his arms on a squeal, she scrambled up the side of the tub and doused the bathroom tiling in the process. Not that he cared if the floor got a little wet; it was well worth it to see that tiny, tawdry silver dress glued to her luscious curves.

Fire gleamed in Taryn's eyes. Her hair hung in sodden black strands. Small lines of mascara marred the undersides of her eyes. She looked amazing.

"Why the—" she sputtered.

He stopped her words short with the tug of a hand on either ankle.

Her fingers shot to the Jacuzzi's rim, gripping like her life depended on it. "Let me go, you jerk!"

"Jerk is it? Would a jerk do this?" Using his grip on her ankle, he lifted her foot from below the water's surface. And then, like an enraged bull, he caught that sexy shade of siren red winking at him from her toenails and charged at his target.

Her heels were off and flung out of the tub in a heartbeat. He was sucking her big toe between his lips in the next. The air whooshed out of Taryn's mouth, followed by an incredibly girlish giggle.

Giggles were good. Just not now. Not when the point was to drive her crazy with lust.

He quit with the sucking to lick the length of her toe, tease the sensitized skin with little nips of his teeth and the circling of his tongue. The giggles turned to whimpers and then moans as he again drew her toe into the wet warmth of his mouth, this time slowly, this time with the lapping of his tongue. This time he added his fingers to the mix, freeing her other ankle to trace his short nails up her damp, bare inner thigh.

Brian walked his fingers to the edge of the dress's tiny skirt and then dipped beneath the drenched material. He held his fingers there, toying near the edge of the scrap of cotton covering her sex, but never touching, never venturing beyond. Taryn's grip on the Jacuzzi's rim increased visibly. Her hips writhed to the suction of his mouth along her toe. In and out. In and out. His cock pulsed with each suggestively erotic move. His balls tightened. All the while he watched her face, watched the stunning passion building in her eyes, over her features.

Her hips shoved forward with the next quick, fast thrust of his mouth. Her lips parted on a sexy sigh. "Touch me. Please."

Ignoring the fact that she was trying to call the shots, trying to control him again, he dutifully did her bidding.

Almost.

Keeping the toying rhythm of his fingers in progress, Brian rose up on his knees to brush his mouth across her bare stomach. The taste of her exploded over his senses. Spicy cinnamon. Silently bold and commanding, like the woman herself.

"Not there." Taryn moaned.

He turned his day-old stubble on her navel, and the urgent push of her fingers into his hair seemed to suggest she'd change her mind. For that he allowed her his thumb, rubbing it against her clit through her panties with each brush of his chin against her belly.

The muscles of her stomach clenched beneath his lips. Her grip on his hair increased. A little wheezing breath left her. "Okay. Maybe there."

With an inward smile, he sank his tongue into her navel, taunted with more of the licks and sucks he'd given her toe, and then followed up with that same damnable in and out thrusting game that was driving his dick to distraction.

The hand between her thighs picked up the pace, mimicking in suit, dipping beneath her panties and into the tightness of her pussy. She bucked off the Jacuzzi's rim with the impaling and then settled into a grinding, greedy pace against his fingers.

"Ooh... Definitely right there." Taryn's words panted out.

And she *was* right there too, Brian knew. A few more licks, a few more sucks, a few more fucks of his finger, and she would be coming. Only he wouldn't allow that tonight. Not this way.

With a last, lingering lick of her navel, he turned the heat of his gaze on her crotch. Her gorgeous cunt was still covered and that would not do another moment.

"Lift up."

Without hesitation, she responded. Lifted her butt off the rim just far enough for him to take hold of the sides of her panties and skim the wet cotton down her shiny wet legs.

Challenge showed in her eyes as she settled back down and spread her thighs. First, by parting her legs. And, second, by moving her hand between her legs and using her first two fingers to part her pussy lips wide.

He groaned with the sight of all that beautiful pink flesh and the bloodred bundle of nerves at the center. She would finger herself if he asked. She would do close to anything he wanted. Right now he didn't want her doing anything. Just sitting back and enjoying the ride.

Brian pushed the hem of the dress to her waist, baring her to the navel. Scooping her ass into his hands, he brought them mouth to pussy. Using the V of her fingers as his divine guide, he sank his tongue into the swollen folds of her labia. Liquid warmth rushed out to meet him. He lapped up her delicious cream like a starving man, or rather a man who knew this could be their last night together.

Taryn's hands returned to his hair, pushed deep, and held on tight. "I can't hold on long when you're doing that."

Good. It was high time she was the one to come quickly. Quickly and hard.

With that mission in mind, he ceased the flicks of his tongue to turn his teeth on her clit. Scraping his teeth over its edges, he freed a butt cheek to stroke his fingers along her crack. The tip of one finger brushed against her anal opening with the move, and she tensed beneath his touch. Pulling her clit between her teeth and nibbling rang the tension back out of her. Right up until the moment, he nudged that same finger into the opening of her anus.

"Brian, I don't think—"

"Then don't. Don't think. Feel. Let go of the control. One more time." He'd never had a woman touch his butt in any manner, but he'd been with more than one who enjoyed anal play. As much as Taryn had gotten into his spankings, she was bound to find great pleasure in the feel of his fingers massaging her asshole.

Wariness stayed in her eyes, but finally she nodded. "For you."

"No," he corrected. "For you."

Returning his head between her legs, he stroked her pussy with his tongue, ate at her with flat, short strokes while his finger gently probed the rim of her anus. Slowly, he sank inside, felt the tight passage first grow taut and then release with his entry. He heightened the flicks of his tongue in time with the push of his finger past her sphincter. Another tensing in his arms, and then a loud, luscious sigh of ecstasy as she melted against his seeking finger.

Brian's cock bobbed anxiously with the release of her control. He curbed his harried want to focus. To keep his tongue and lips pleasuring her sweet pussy while his fingers continued on their hedonistic journey. He found her clit again, pressed his tongue flat and hard against the bead. Her sigh this time was hard, needful. Her hips no longer lay dormant, her body prone in his arms, but picked up a restless bucking tempo, grinding her cunt against his feasting lips with each forward thrust and his finger deeper into her slickening passage with each backward one.

That's it, babe. Give in. Ride the wave.

As if she heard the silent encouragement, Taryn increased the pace, hammering her butt against his palms, taking his finger deeper still. Lust coursed through his veins, hot and heavy and desperate for relief. He denied himself that pleasure, only to find an even greater one as he pulled her clit between his lips and suckled hard.

"I'm going to...come."

The words all but sobbed from her lips. Seconds later, she went still and her hot cream flooded his tongue. And then she was moving again, her buttocks shoving back hard, devouring his finger again and again, her pussy weeping for entry of its own.

Near painfully, her fingers dug into his head. "I need...you...inside."

Before he could think to respond, her hands released from his hair and she shoved hard at his shoulders. Taken by surprise, he fell backward in the water. When he regained his stance on his knees, it was to find her turned around, her dress shed, and her stomach resting on the Jacuzzi's edge. With her legs spread wide, she wiggled her bare ass tauntingly in his face while her soaked pussy provided a wide-open rear view worthy of all-out devotion.

Brian's attention darted back to her butt as her intentions took hold. His balls squeezed tight. She couldn't mean... "What are you doing?"

"Losing control." Her voice was thick yet breathy, sated yet eager. It tore at his fleeting control, but not nearly so much as her amendment of, "Giving up control. I want to feel your cock in my ass."

His throat went parchment dry, and he swallowed convulsively. What she was giving him was more than he'd ever have thought to ask for, but it was also everything he craved, now that the offer was out there. Still, he had to give her the chance to change her mind... before he was balls-deep in her silky asshole and unable to comprehend the meaning of stop. "Are you sure?"

"Never more."

Primal instinct had him ready to grab hold and thrust home. Common sense had him stepping out of the Jacuzzi.

"Don't leave me." Her words came out half plea, half sob.

Brian couldn't curb his rough laugh. "Trust me, Taryn, leaving is the last thing on my mind." Quickly going to the sink, he grabbed a condom and the small tube of moisturizer from his bathroom bag. Not his first choice of lubricants, but mixed with her natural lube, it would work just fine. He sheathed himself in seconds and then showed her the moisturizer as he climbed back into the tub. "Making you feel good is the first."

She threw a smile at him over her shoulder. One that was thick with as much anticipation as there was uncertainty.

He moved back onto his knees and came up behind her to gently caress her butt. She would not regret this decision. No, she would spend the rest of her life remembering it for all the right reasons.

A touch of his mouth along the sweet spot of her neck brought a shiver coursing through her. Smiling, he rubbed the backs of his fingers along her crack. "Have I mentioned what a gorgeous ass you have?"

"A *big*, gorgeous ass." Insecurity clung to her voice.

"Not big; round. Perfect." Assurance was critical now more than ever.

Lightly coating his finger with the moisturizer, he eased it along her crack and then ever so slowly into her anus. Taryn had taken this same finger fast and hard moments before, and clearly she wanted that same now. The lunging shove of her hips was all the encouragement he needed. He probed his finger the remainder of the way into her opening, coating her interior walls with the moisturizer. The addition of a second coated finger tightened her cheeks. Love bites along her neck vanquished that tensing on a throaty whimper.

Brian moved the digits together inside her asshole, fingering her with long, languorous strokes, until she writhed in his arms, panting, "More. Now. Please."

After ensuring his knees were solid on the Jacuzzi's slippery floor, he brought his free hand around to cup a breast. Kneading the heavy mound, he breathed hotly against her ear, "How much more? Where do you want me?"

"In my butt. I want your cock in my ass. Now, Brian. Before I implode."

Her desperate pleas were almost more than he could take. He pulled his fingers from her ass to take his bobbing dick in hand. He freed her breast long enough to apply a liberal amount of moisturizer to his cock and then guided it to her anal opening.

Her breath caught audibly with the nudge of the thick head against her anus. He paused to regain his hold on her breast and lick a salty-sweet path along her neck. The end of that path found her ear again, where he issued a hot, hungry, "Ready?"

Her answer was a nod. He took her at that. Took hold of the root of his cock and slowly fed the length into the rosette of her asshole. And, fuck, was she tight. His entire body spasmed with the highly sensual slide of his dick. He bit down hard on her neck with the intense pressure, then harder as he found resistance at her sphincter. He shoved past as gently as possible.

Taryn froze in his arms, squeaking out an "Oh."

Not quite balls-deep yet. He could stop. Hell, he could stop even when he was balls-deep. He just didn't want to.

Disappointment curling his gut, Brian asked, "Stop?"

"No. Go. Slowly."

Relief sailed through him. Loving a nipple with playful tweaks, he carefully eased deeper, then deeper still, pausing each time she went a little tense, or made a sound that didn't quite fit pleasure. And then he was finally there, buried to the hilt, home sweet home.

Mother of God did it feel like heaven.

He'd never quite been down his path before. Never felt anything so tight and right as her asshole enveloping him, the demanding press of her nipple against his palm. Never heard anything so erotic as her breathless sigh of, "Yes... Fuck me."

He was also never more eager to accept an invitation.

Taking both breasts in his hands, he squeezed her rock-hard nipples while his cock moved within her butt. Slowly at first and then faster. Faster yet with their heightening pants, and the glorious sound and feel of his balls pummeling her wet pussy from behind.

"Oh my... I feel like my butt is going to explode," Taryn cried out, her fingers going white-knuckle on the Jacuzzi's rim, her butt meeting him thrust for desperate thrust. "Don't you dare stop! It's good. So *sooo* good."

No, she was good. Too damned good to let him do this after all that had gone down. But he wasn't complaining. And he sure as hell wasn't stopping. He might be coming, though, and damned soon at that.

Brian released a breast to slide his hand between the small space between her and the Jacuzzi's side. Opening her cunt with the tip of his finger, he parted her lips and found her engorged clit. With each of their joint thrusts, he petted the tender pearl, and with each pet, she gasped out her throaty approval. With the next shove, she clenched her buttocks tightly around his cock.

The move came out of nowhere and took him over. His orgasm pounded at his ears, barreled along his spine, and yanked at his balls. He ceased the casual pets to squeeze, twist, pinch the nubbin, and then to drive two fingers into her pussy.

Taryn exploded with the entry. Her cunt clenched his finger fiercely, and honey showered over his hand. The muscles of her anus tightened again with her release. He could no longer hold back if his life were at stake. He came hard, pounding his dick into her ass, again and again, until he felt like breathing was too great a chore and then he simply held on to her, clung to her back, and relied on her to bear both of their weights as he rode out the overwhelming climax.

"For...me..." Taryn's satisfied words sounded a moment later.

It took another few seconds for Brian to drag his weight off her. She went instantly liquid in his arms, giving him her full weight in return. All too gladly, he pulled her back to his chest. He moved them to the far edge of the Jacuzzi, separating his softening cock from the sweetness of her ass in the process.

That he would probably never again experience sex of any kind with her hit hard. And then it was forgotten as she turned in his arms to slant her mouth across his. She kissed him with slow, drugging speed. And he kissed her back with all the sensations rocketing through him. Her fingers found his arms to stroke leisurely, and he felt that way now, seconds after flying so high. Calm and content, more than happy to stay like this for another hour, or day. Or, hell, weeks.

She got to you, buddy. Got to you good.

As if she knew his thoughts and feared them, Taryn pulled away from his kiss and then his arms and lap. She sank back against the Jacuzzi's side and stared at him speechlessly. He stared back. Time passed. Seconds. Minutes. Tension grew out of the silence. He searched his mind for words and found none worthy of speaking, or at least that she would want to hear. They were temporary friends at best. Not speaking their minds was the only safe option.

It was she who finally broke the silence. A teasing smile curving her lips, she glanced down in the water at the direction of his groin. "You never did tell me his name. You said it wasn't Willy."

Brian grinned back over the easy, playful topic. "It isn't. It's Bobo."

They shared in a laugh that evaporated the tension. When the sound died away, Taryn inquired, "Are you serious?"

He nodded. "I named him when I was three. My vocabulary was too limited at the time to come up with King Kong the Monkey Slayer."

"What a shame too."

He thought she would laugh again. Instead, the humor faded from her eyes. She moved to the other side of the Jacuzzi and stood. The sight of her bare, beautiful body made him want her all over again.

Before he could grab for her, she stepped over the side of the tub. "It's late, and I want to be in the room when Sarah arrives."

Brian paused with the familiar name. "Sarah? As in your best friend Sarah?"

"Yeah." She pulled a towel from the nearby rack to blot at her hair. "She showed up tonight. Laurel, this Wiccan we're doing some promo work with and who is somewhat of a friend of ours, got this vibe, or vision, or something, about my needing Sarah with me before I burst from negative energy. So Sarah being Sarah came to Sugar Foot."

"She is where exactly?" Taryn leaving her friend alone after Sarah had come all this way to see her was both shocking and strange. It suggested Taryn either liked Brian more than she'd let on, or liked her friend less than he'd imagined.

"Trying to trap Mike Carmichael into admitting he's been sleeping with conference attendees."

All question over Taryn's motives vanished with his aghast, "*What*?"

She frowned. "Yeah, I know. I was shocked too, but I saw him. I didn't know it was him at the time—he was wearing a wig—but still I saw him getting down and dirty with one woman and then with his tongue stuck down some other woman's throat the next day. The guy is a major sleaze."

Instantaneous temper bolted through him. "A sleaze Sarah is now alone with?" he demanded. He didn't know Mike well, but the few times he'd talked with the man, Brian had always been glad to see the conversation end. "What the hell were you thinking to let her go off alone with him?"

She stopped blotting at her hair. Her frown deepened as if she was just catching on to the fact that he wasn't thrilled by this news. "She said she'd be fine. That she'd call me if she got into trouble."

"Yeah, unless she can't call, because Mike has her tied down and is punishing her for trying to blow his cover. That was a stupid move, Taryn!" His anger was running rampant, his words edged with scorn, but damn it, he couldn't help it.

What if Sarah hadn't come along? Would Taryn have thrown herself at Mike? He couldn't think about that without feeling sick. "What do you hope to gain by exposing Mike, just to get other women thrown out of the conference? The whole misery loves company deal?"

"No! Sarah is doing it so that I can get back in."

"Mike doesn't have that power. He doesn't even have as much power as I do, and I couldn't get you back in. I told you I tried. I did everything I could think of and more."

"Well..." Taryn looked away, as if searching for a viable excuse, then back at him, her eyebrows drawn together. "Sarah said he could get power, that with the right motivation he could accomplish anything."

"Sarah's wrong, and from the sounds of things, lacks common sense."

She gasped. "Sarah is smart, you idiot. She's also one of the only real friends I have, so don't you dare sit there and talk bad about her."

"One of your *only* real friends? What happened to all those huggy, lovey friends you claimed to have last night? Or were they made up like all those things you made up that first day you saw me in order to make yourself look better, more stable, more in control?"

The gasp was back, followed by a hurt look that cut directly to Brian's soul. She blinked at him, and he thought she might cry. Then her eyes narrowed to icy blue slits. "I was almost right before when I said there's a very good chance that I hate you. Almost, because there isn't any chance about it."

Before he could respond, she was grabbing her dress and rushing out of the bathroom and, if the slamming of a door was any sign, out of his hotel room completely.

* * *

"I really am sorry, Tare," Sarah implored with a poignant little smile that might have an effect on the male libido, but was lost on Taryn. "I thought it would work. But, hey, look on the bright side, at least you aren't the only one out of the conference for breaking the rules."

Taryn burrowed farther under the covers, immersing herself completely, and tried to see the bright side in that. Outside of the obvious—Sarah returning safely—there was no bright side.

Five other women had been tossed out of the conference for sleeping with Mike. Those women didn't even know it yet. Sarah had blackmailed Mike into going to Shewson's room at two in the morning to admit what he'd done. Shewson assured them he would take action at first light, in the form of expunging the women from the conference. It was after three now, another four hours or so and, thanks to Taryn agreeing with Sarah's plan, five women's dreams would be destroyed.

Yep, bright side. Just call her sunshine girl.

"So, you still haven't answered my question," Sarah said. "How did you get your dress wet? And don't tell me you spilled something on it. The whole thing— well, what little there is to it—is drenched."

Taryn heaved a sigh against a mouthful of sheets. Why bother lying? Her encounter with Brian went with the rest of this day completely. In other words, it sucked. Okay, so not the first part of their encounter, but the end of it sucked with a capital *S*. "I went to see Brian."

"I think you said you went to see Brian, but you might have said 'I went to pee, crying.' It's really hard to tell with those covers over your head."

She *so* did not want to laugh. But apparently that was what best friends were for—making you laugh when life dealt you crap. Taryn gave in to a quick laugh, which managed to relieve some of her belly pain. That is, until she spoke. "Brian pulled me into his Jacuzzi with my clothes on."

"Okay, that I heard. And what happened?"

Too much. He'd made her feel more than sexy and sensual and like she'd never come so hard in her life as when his cock had been buried in her ass. He'd made her feel…something else. Something probably not good.

As much as ending the night by arguing was not Taryn's idea of a fun time, it was still better than what might have happened if she had stayed. The kiss they shared after their mutually massive orgasms had been hugely intense. Not in a sexual way, either. Rather in an emotional way that had reached deep down inside her and made her want to share all her secrets. And that was not good.

"He gave me a screaming orgasm, we fought over you, I told him I hate him, and I left."

Sarah whipped back the covers. A frown knit her forehead. "Oh, honey, you fought over me—about what?"

Taryn blinked. Bright lights. Worse, she had to finish this without the covers to hide behind. Now would be a really good time for Brian to show up with a pint of Chocolate Cashew Heaven.

She should be pissed at him, never wanting to see him again. Instead, she was wishing he were here. That had the makings of messy written all over it. "He said it was stupid of you to go off alone with Mike, that it wouldn't matter if you got him to tell the truth, because Mike has less influence on this conference than Brian does, and he'd already tried everything he could to get me back in."

Sarah looked thoughtful for a moment, then, "He has a point. Not that I'm stupid, but it didn't help you out, and I wasted the perfect opportunity to meet lucky guy number seven." She smiled knowingly. "And you don't hate him, Tare. Unless he's blind, he's got to be able to see how you really feel."

How she *really* felt? How was that?

Never mind. She didn't want to know.

"It doesn't matter if I hate him or not. We're going home in less than thirty-six hours. We live hundreds of miles apart and probably will never see each other again. Besides, I don't even care. It isn't like he means anything to me. So he thinks my latest lyrics are great and says he believes in me. So what? Lots of people do."

Sarah quirked a blonde eyebrow. "Lots?"

"You do."

"Of course I do. I'm your best friend and have a great ear for music, but not lots, Taryn. Not even your parents."

"Gee, thanks for reminding me. It's my dad that's the problem. Mom's just...Mom. He talks, she agrees."

As much as Taryn used to think her mother believed in her and wanted to see her follow her dreams, her mother hadn't even put up a marginal fight when her father withdrew her college tuition money after learning she was studying songwriting. So many others had done the same to her, turned their backs on her in one form or another when it came to pursuing her dream. Only Sarah truly believed in her, and now Brian. Brian whom she didn't hate, but after the way she treated him so badly yet again, he probably did hate her.

"I need sleep." Taryn yanked the covers back over her head.

"All right, but promise me something."

"What?"

"When you're dreaming about Brian and screaming orgasms tonight, keep it quiet. I'm still upset about missing out on lucky guy number seven, and I'm going to be jealous as hell if you start moaning."

Chapter Twenty

If there was something good to be said about not falling asleep until after four in the morning, it was that Taryn slept in till noon. It was well past the time the showcase performers would begin.

She could have gone and watched. Still could, since the performances would last for several hours. But while yesterday afternoon Taryn had been able to accept that she'd blown her chance of winning a conference contract and would have to find another way to break into the industry, today she wasn't stomaching it so well. Today, as Sarah pulled the drapes that covered the glass doors leading to the balcony and sunlight burst into the room, all Taryn wanted to do was burrow to the bottom of the bed and forget she'd ever woken up.

Better yet, forget she'd ever decided to come to Sugar Foot.

If she'd passed on the once-in-a-lifetime conference invitation, she would have always been disgusted with herself. But at least she wouldn't have felt this painful burning sensation in the pit of her belly that felt way too much like failure.

"Rise and shine, hon," Sarah sang out, a wide smile curving her lips. "The sun's up, and the beach is full of bronzed, beautiful island hotties just waiting for a piece of Taryn the Songwriting Goddess."

Ugh! As if Sarah's chipper morning attitude wasn't bad enough...

Taryn squinted through the sunlight at her friend, who was dressed in a miniscule red bikini, matching Prada sandals, and black sunglasses. "I think you mistook me for another Taryn. This version would be the Songwriting Flop."

"Your songs didn't flop, Tare; they never even had a chance to be heard. Not by anyone but Brian anyway, and you said he loved them."

Brian. Another point of failure for this week.

Taryn had managed to start the week out loathing him and believing he was a jerk, and end it by acting like a jerk herself, and more than likely, made him loathe her because of it. Yeah, burrowing to the end of the bed held real promise. "He didn't love the old stuff. He said it was nice but lacked passion."

"Fine, then the new stuff. You said he thought it was great. Obviously it was passionate too, for him to have given such high praise. He was already in your pants at that time, so it isn't like he said it to score points on that end."

He had been in her pants from the day she arrived on the island, almost from the hour. Then there was the fact that he'd been honest with her in saying her music was only nice earlier in the week, so he had to have been as sincere when he said it was great these last couple days.

Great music she would never get to share with anyone other than Brian and Sarah. Peachy.

Groaning, Taryn rolled onto her stomach, pulled the covers up to her neck, and closed her eyes.

"What are you doing?" Sarah demanded.

"Tired," she mumbled against a pillow.

"You're not tired. You're just acting like a big chickenshit again." Sarah's voice went from scolding to concerned. "What is it with you, girl? I swear ever since you got the invitation to this conference, I've barely known who you are. It sure as heck isn't the confident, go-getting Taryn James who promised the day we started up Lasting Impressions that it was a short-term venture on her part, because soon she'd be living her dreams."

Oh, now that was low-down, throwing that reminder in Taryn's face. If she had any energy, she would roll back over and give Sarah a piece of her mind. Best friend, ha!

"I get that being booted from the conference was painful. But so what?" Sarah continued. "You're stronger than that. Better than that. You're better than lying in bed moping all day too. I love you, Tare. I believe in you. You've told me more than once that Brian believes in you. That's two of us, and I guarantee if you keep trying, you'll see there's a whole lot more fans out there. Now, as much as I'd love to stay inside and continue this one-sided conversation, I only have one more day left in paradise, and I plan to take advantage of it."

The closing of the hotel room door rang through Taryn's head with a resounding sense of finality. The end of her dream. The end of her friendship with

Sarah. It could have been either of those if she chose it. Taryn refused to do so.

Sarah was right. She was being pathetic. Completely unlike herself.

But Sarah was also wrong. The invitation to this conference wasn't what put her personality change into motion. The conference had merely been the impetus that brought forth old insecurities. The fear of seeing Brian again had done that, as well. They both represented the same thing, being judged. Possibly being found lacking, being told she wasn't good enough to make it, to achieve her dream.

Her fears where Brian was concerned had turned out to be complete nonsense. If it weren't for being dismissed from the conference, her fears there likely would have proved to be just as ridiculous.

She *had* been dismissed, but like Sarah had said, so what? There were other venues to getting her songs in front of those with the power to see that they went somewhere. Somehow she'd get her songs in front of those people, and the lyrics would connect so completely, passing them over would not be an option. And also like Sarah had said, Taryn only had one more day left in paradise, and she'd be damned if she wasn't taking advantage of it.

Feeling revived and more assured of herself than she'd been in weeks, Taryn slipped from the bed and headed for the bathroom. Shower. Shave. Finish the song she'd begun this week. And then later, when she could hope that Brian would be finished with his conference duties and back in his room, she'd return to the paradise she'd been aching for since leaving him last night.

* * *

Brian turned on the TV and flopped back on the bed. Today had been a long, tiring day, which started too early and ended with Serena giving him another chance to accept her no-strings-attached, one-night-of-sex offer.

He'd been tempted. Not physically, but mentally.

If anything was going to kill the hunger for Taryn that had been thick in his blood since she'd left him last night, it had to be sleeping with another woman. He'd been sure he was going to tell Serena yes. Then he opened his mouth and out came "thanks, but no thanks." Not long after that he'd dragged his sorry ass back to his room. And here he sat, watching an unrecognizable movie at nine o'clock on a Saturday night in the middle of a tropical paradise.

Hell, he had to get her out of his head.

Today had been too hectic to even consider tracking Taryn down. Tomorrow he hoped to catch her before his noon flight took off. Last time they parted, it had been on the same unstable terms they were currently on. That instability bothered Brian on and off through the years. It bothered Taryn far more. This time he had a feeling that leaving things as is would bother them both too much to forget.

Tomorrow he would seek her out, give her one last bumbling apology for losing his temper—even if it was for good reason—and say good-bye. Most likely forever.

The impact of the thought knotted his gut. Damn, he didn't want that.

He dragged a hand through his hair and blew out a breath. A casual good-bye was not going to cut it with Taryn. If he was going to get her out of his head and feel like things between them ended on a good note, he needed to do something more. Something—

A loud knock cut him off, followed by, "Brian? Are you in there?"

The familiar sound of her voice brought an immediate smile to his face. He leaped off the bed and went to the door, pulling it open. He paused then, at the sight of her standing in his doorway. She wasn't wearing that sinfully snug little red wrapper from their first night together, or the impossibly tiny, tawdry silver dress from last night. She had on frayed jean shorts and a dark blue, loose-fitting tank top. Her silky black hair was pulled back in a ponytail, and her sun-kissed face clean of so much as lipstick.

She looked incredible.

"Hey." Brian somehow resisted the urge to pull her into his arms.

"Hey," Taryn returned, a smile curving her lips that looked innocent, but the hardening effect it had on his cock suggested it wasn't innocent in the least. She pushed past him into the hotel room. "I hope you don't mind..."

Her scent wrapped around him as she moved. Today it was light, earthy, and yet somehow every bit as powerful as the hot cinnamon scent he'd licked from her body several times.

He closed the door and turned back to find her standing in the same place she'd stopped last night, directly in front of the bathroom door. The difference was that last night, at least before he goaded her into joining him in the Jacuzzi, she seemed shifty about being in his room. Today she seemed at ease.

"You're always welcome at my place," he assured her.

"You might not think so after the way I've been acting, but the same goes for you." Taryn's expression turned earnest. "Last night was incredible. And then I ruined it with stupidity. I'm sorry."

Brian hadn't put much thought into why she'd come to his room until right now. If he'd have guessed, he would have said to blame him for Sarah's reckless plan not working out. He wouldn't have guessed she'd come to apologize. And certainly not so sincerely. "It was my fault as much as yours. I shouldn't have—"

"Fine, we can share the guilt. The point is, that was last night and we can't get it back. This is our last night on Sugar Foot, and I want to spend it with you." Heat simmered into her eyes. She held out a hand. "The whole night, Brian. Is that all right? For the record, yes would be the right answer here."

As if he could say no.

Not only was every ounce of him aching to have her again, but sharing a last night together was exactly what he needed to be able to say good-bye without regret. One night where they weren't arguing about stupid shit or fighting about control or anything else. Just one night of being them.

Grinning, he took her hand and tugged her to him, until the softness of her big breasts rubbed against his chest. "What do you think?"

She laughed. "I'll take that as a yes."

His blood fired with the sexy, full-bodied laugh. Even if he could manage to forget Taryn, he had a feeling her laugh would stay with him the rest of his life. "That would be a hell yes, woman."

Brian lowered his mouth and rubbed her lips lightly. Taryn's arms snaked around his neck, but she didn't attempt to take over, just brushed her lips back and held on to him. Slowly, the kiss deepened from soft caresses to gentle exploring and teasing nips. And then throaty little moans from her throat and answering deeper ones from his as their tongues met and danced. The slow movements quickened until there was no denying the burning ache between them, or the unstoppable desire that had stolen over the moment.

He could go on kissing her, inhaling her sweet scent, consuming her luscious lips and husky little mewls for hours. But he wanted to do that while buried deep inside her. With a last kiss, he lifted her arms from his neck. He took one of her hands in his and led her to the bed. She kicked off her flip-flops and followed him soundlessly. He let free her hand when they reached the bed, and she murmured, "I need you now."

"I need you too," he admitted, his voice thick with more than lust.

Brian knew they couldn't last in the long run, and yet he couldn't shut out the feelings she evoked in him. Here, tonight, he wouldn't. If revealing the emotions she stirred in him scared her, it was a risk he would take.

He unbuttoned his dress shirt and pushed the sleeves off his shoulders. Hungry, dark blue eyes trained on him, she pulled her tank top over her head to reveal a lacy black bra. Her nipples stabbed against the material, making his mouth water to taste them.

He moved to his belt, unbuckling it and pulling it from the loops of his pants with a quick tug. The leather lashed out, cracking the air, and Taryn blinked and licked her lower lip. Brian licked his own lips as she unbuttoned her jean shorts and slid them down her tanned legs. Her panties matched the black lace of her bra, and telltale wetness darkened the triangle between her thighs.

Guessing her pussy was wet for him and knowing it was were two different things. His breathing quickened while his dick throbbed. His hands shook as he hurried to remove the rest of his clothes. Finally, he was as naked as she was, down to his underwear.

She looked to his solid cock, desperately trying to escape his briefs. Her smile was huge as she stepped forward and wrapped her arms around his waist. "I think Bobo's happy to see me."

He chuckled and bent for a kiss. "I'd say Bobo's ecstatic to see you." He'd also say Bobo was going to miss her a hell of a lot come morning.

Brian pushed that thought aside and lifted her into his arms and onto the bed. Coming down beside her, he pulled the ponytail holder from her hair. Inky black waves cascaded around her face and onto the top edges of her breasts.

He captured a fistful of locks and brushed the ends over the straining tip of a nipple through her bra.

She shivered. "Don't tease. I want you for real. Now. And not because I'm a sexual control freak who can't wait any longer. I could if I wanted to. Probably."

He laughed at the uncertainty tacked onto the end, able to relate well. "I think we've broken you of that nasty little sexual control freak habit. And I can't wait any longer, either. My dick's been half-hard since you left last night."

"Sorry about that."

"Don't be. You're going to make it up right now." Grabbing her around the waist, he rolled onto his back, taking her with him.

Taryn sat back to straddle him. "What do you say to an oral apology?"

"Maybe later." He reached for her bra straps, sliding them off her shoulders and down her arms. Using the straps as a pry, he pulled the bra down a little, so that the cups slipped away to expose the top of her areolas. He thumbed the sensitive flesh. "Right now I want you to ride me."

Oohing in appreciation, she arched into his touch and brought her erect nipples brushing along his thumbs. "I want that. I want us naked, you inside me."

"Take me then."

She didn't hesitate, but moved quickly down his body. He lifted his hips when she gave his briefs a tug and then stripped them down his legs. She eyed his long, hard dick, and it bobbed with the heat of her gaze.

"Better keep going," he warned. "Knowing how speedy Bobo tends to be around you, he's liable to go off with just a look."

Taryn looked up and laughed. "I thought his quick to the finish problem was my fault?"

"Maybe, or maybe you excite me too much to contain myself."

"I think it's the other way around." She skimmed her panties down her legs. Straddling his pelvis, she taunted his sex with the damp slide of her own "You make me wet, Brian. Wetter than I ever remember being. You make my pussy ache so badly, I need to touch it."

His breath halted in anticipation. She reached between her legs, skimming his cock en route to her destination. He trembled with the touch. Then trembled even harder when she stroked her pussy lips, in and out, and over the swollen bundle of nerves hidden between them. When he would have joined in, she gave him a playful smile and stopped the show.

But only long enough to venture to a new location.

Taryn unhooked her bra and tossed it aside. She took her breasts in hand before he could make that same move. With a decadent sigh, she stroked the mounds, and then concentrated on rolling and squeezing the hard buds that centered them. "You make my nipples so stiff I can't stop from playing with them."

And she made his dick so hard, if she didn't stop soon, he seriously would be ending things on a hasty note. "Taryn."

"Yes?"

"What happened to no teasing?"

She flashed an impish smile. "Oops. Guess I got distracted. I'm not anymore."

Hands on his chest, she lowered herself and brushed his mouth with hers, wiggled her hips against his. The wetness of her pussy nudged against the head of his cock, and he grunted at the sweet ecstasy of skin on skin. No matter how or where he took Taryn, it always felt like the greatest of sensual treats.

"I want you inside me now, Brian. I want to make love with you."

"Definitely," he managed, his mind spinning with what she'd called their actions—for once not sex or any other euphemism for lovemaking—and took her mouth with a fierce kiss.

Rocking against him, she kissed him back with fervor, meeting his tongue lick for hungry lick, suck for salacious suck. Brian fumbled blindly in the nightstand drawer, where he'd placed the condoms he'd bought earlier in the week in the hopes of a night like this. Last night he hadn't believed they'd ever again come to this pass.

Tonight...tonight he was just trying not to come, period.

His fingers connected with the box, and he jerked it out. He moved from her mouth to her neck, nibbling at that spot below her ear that never ceased to drive her crazy. And it accomplished just that.

Her hands moved wildly over his body. The rasp of her nails ignited every nerve ending he possessed, while her hips writhed and thrust against him until it was all he could do not to push inside her, skin against skin.

He attempted to put the condom on while alternately licking and blowing on her neck, but her wriggling wouldn't allow for it. Lifting from her neck, he said, "Condom."

Taryn sat back. At first she looked dazed, then she focused on the foil packet in his hand and smiled. "Good thinking."

She took the packet, ripping it open with her teeth. She made quick work of rolling it on and then she was back, lowering her chest to his, rubbing her breasts against him, her pelvis against his.

She nipped a kiss at the corner of his mouth. "Ready?"

"More than."

With a husky laugh, she sank onto the hard length of his cock. Her laughter died to a moan, and her hands came up to his shoulders, gripping. His moan followed as the feel of her pussy muscles taking him to the hilt rocketed through him. Again it hit him that it didn't matter how or where he had her; it always felt so damned good, so right. It always made him want to go faster than he dared.

Taryn was shockingly still for an instant. Then she leaned back far enough to have her breasts inches from his face and rode him like a champion. Sensations rushed through him with each push in and pull out of her slick pussy. Sensations that turned to emotions as her brilliant blue gaze connected with his. Everything about her was so open now, so free.

So easy to love.

Brian blinked against the thought. He'd seen it coming, known she'd gotten to him good, and still the knowledge that he'd fallen for her was like a sucker punch. This couldn't last; they both knew it. She'd said it more than once.

Shutting off that portion of his feelings, he focused on the physical, concentrated on the way her body hugged his close, the heat in her eyes. The urgency in her kiss as she lowered to his mouth and consumed him with fast, hungry licks, and then erratic sucks as her body clamped tightly around his.

Her orgasm was a wild rush, a frenzy of warmth and wetness and cries of ecstasy. His followed seconds behind, rippling through him and shaking him to the core. Unlike Taryn, he didn't cry out. Not because he didn't want to, but because he didn't trust the words that would leave his mouth.

Chapter Twenty-one

Taryn lay against Brian's warm body, hugging him close, never wanting to leave this bed again. Of course she had to. Not now, but in the morning, when the plane would take her back to reality.

Now she could put that reality off just a bit longer, the same way she was struggling to do with her feelings. Sarah had said last night it was obvious how she felt for Brian. Taryn had questioned how that was. Now she knew, and now she knew she could never put it into words.

She could attempt to learn a bit more about him one last time, though, mementos to take with her. She kissed his chest and lifted her head to smile up at him. "I know we can't last beyond tomorrow, but I want to know about you, Brian. I want to know the real you. Please."

"I never should have made you beg that first time. You've gotten way too good at it for me to say no."

His lazy smile said he wouldn't have said no even if she hadn't said please. Her heart squeezed tight with the knowledge, and she rested her head back on his chest, waiting for him to talk.

"I'm not a corporate raider or shark, or whatever it was you called me the other day. Anything you've ever read or heard said about me made it sound that way, because I wanted it to seem that way." He hesitated a beat, then added in a quieter voice, "Life's easier when you don't have any close connections."

Easier maybe, but hardly worth living. As much as her relationship wasn't always perfect with her parents, she still made it a point to visit them every few weeks or so. "That guy and his wife at Maria's seemed pretty close."

"I helped them out before Mom passed away."

The sad note in his voice couldn't have been missed. Taryn had wanted to know about his mother for so long, about how she'd died. Now she fought over pressing the issue and forgetting about it, for fear rehashing it would be too painful on him. She settled on letting Brian be the one to decide how much to tell. "So you changed after she died?"

"Yeah. From what you said before, you obviously know a lot about my family...about Mom not having anyone to support her. My dad's the kind of guy who needs attention. Mom gave him all she could, but focusing on her career took a lot of time, too much for Dad. When I was born, she had that much less time to give him, and he reacted by leaving us. I didn't see that much of him growing up, which is probably how I ended up so close with my mom."

His voice drew quiet, tight at the end, and he inhaled audibly before continuing. "Mom didn't die overnight, the way the press made out. She'd been sick for a long time, months. She had hepatitis C. If she'd given up singing and focused on her health, she might still be alive, but she wouldn't be happy."

Taryn's belly tightened with old ache for him. She'd known from the lone time she'd seen him with his mother that they'd been close. She also could understand what he meant now. "Because her music career was her life. You too, of course, but you were part of her career in a lot of ways, by being there for her, at her concerts whenever possible and helping with her songs and stuff."

"Yeah." Brian's hand came to her back and moved in slow circles. Minutes passed before he spoke again. "I was dating Serena at the time Mom first took sick. I thought she was everything I'd ever wanted. Then I found out about Mom's illness, and I realized how short life really is, and how much Serena wasn't what I wanted. Oh, she's great, don't get me wrong, easy to get along with, agrees to just about anything, and her aspirations are fine, but they fall far short of anything you might call a dream."

"Not your ideal woman."

"Not at all. So I got rid of her. A few months later, Mom died." His voice returned to the low, unsteady tone, and his hand paused on her back. "You don't realize how close someone is to you until you lose them. Since Mom hadn't spoken with her parents in years, and my dad was hardly ever around, she was my only family. When I lost her, I...I guess I hardened my heart."

How awful for him. Not that Taryn was a walking example of a person who gave love easily, but that was about principle, not past heartbreak. "So no one can get close enough to you to hurt you," she said softly.

"It's easier that way, like I said."

"Easier, but not really living." She looked up at him, unsurprised to see the weighty look in his eyes. What she would pay to make it go away. "You can't tell me you enjoy going through life pretending to be a hard-ass and not having any real friends."

Brian looked thoughtful for a second and then grinned. "I don't know. I'd say there's a lot to be said for temporary friendships."

Taryn wanted to smile back, to feel giddy about this temporary relationship they'd forged, but too much was on her mind, not the least of which was that tomorrow their relationship would end. "So, if you aren't this hard-ass corporate shark, what do you really do?"

His grin faded to a smile that spoke of satisfaction in his career choice. "Generally I go in and help a company restructure. Depending on how badly the place is doing, they might start back up under another name, which I guess is where the buyout and resell for a profit perception came from. Rarely do I buy out a company and resell it for a profit. When I do, it's at the owner's full discretion, and they reap the rewards from the sale, not me."

Amazing how wrong she'd been about him all these years. She'd already learned how wrong she'd been about him physically. Now, she recognized everything else she thought she knew about him was nothing more than hearsay. "You're a really nice guy, Brian. You shouldn't hide that fact."

His shoulder moved beneath her in a shrug. "Maybe. Maybe not."

"Hey, that's my evasion technique!"

"It's also your turn to share," he said soberly. "Tell me about you. Why do you doubt your songwriting abilities? Why were you afraid to write with your heart until I influenced you to a point you couldn't hold the words in any longer?"

After all that he'd told her, Taryn owed him the answers. Truthfully, she found that she wanted to give them to him. "I told you I respect what your mom did. For years no one believed in her, and yet she rose above that and accomplished so much. That's me. Not that I've accomplished so much, but the rest of it. Not even my parents believe in me."

"Then they don't recognize talent, not the way Sarah and I do. And I wouldn't say you've accomplished so little, either. You co-own a business, sold—what did you say that first day, a gazillion award-winning commercial jingles?—and you're here. To get an invitation to this conference takes dedication and skill. It didn't work out for you, but it doesn't matter. You're going to make it, Taryn, and soon."

Her heart gave a little bump. She wanted to believe him so badly when he looked at her that way, like he knew her so well he couldn't be wrong. "I hope so."

"Don't hope, make it happen. Believe in yourself."

"I will. I do. I promise."

"You'd better"—the sexy grin that always did her in took over his face—"because if I hear so much as a whisper through the industry grapevine about you giving up, I'll track you down and spank your ass until I have you writing again."

She shifted her hips against his, smiling when she felt his cock awaken, hard and fast, against her inner thigh. "Mmm... I do like it when you spank me. Your taking control seems very conducive to my creating great lines."

"Like this?"

Brian had her pinned beneath him before she could blink. His mouth was on hers just as fast, feasting, devouring. Consuming her whole. His hands moved over her body, brushing, stroking, palming her breasts and pinching her nipples. Then lower still to sink a finger into her supple body.

Just that fast, passion took her over. Taryn arched against his finger, wanting it deeper, buried all the way to her core. Only not his finger, his body. His heart. "Make love with me, Brian."

"Yes," he murmured against her lips.

He left her long enough to retrieve a fresh condom. He rolled it on and then pushed inside her without hesitation. Their gasps sounded in unison, and then there were only ragged breaths, the sensual slide of hands and limbs, the slapping of damp flesh as their mouths and bodies rocked together.

Too quickly, climax crashed through Taryn. Every other time she'd had sex, she'd been anxious to get to the main event, to achieve orgasm. This time, this moment she wanted the buildup to last forever, at least the whole night. It couldn't, because she was already falling over the edge. And apparently so was Brian, as his release came fast on the heels of hers.

When they were breathing normally again, he rolled them over, so she lay with her head on his chest. He wrapped his arms around her and held on tightly.

Long seconds passed with neither saying a word. Then Brian said quietly near her ear, "I'll always believe in you, Taryn. You're going to go all the way. One of these days soon, I'll be listening to the radio when they say your name, and I'll know right where you are. At home, in bed, with your lover."

Oh, God. This was not a nice feeling she was experiencing. Nuh-uh. Not nice at all. And how was it possible to go from moaning with bliss to wanting to cry with heartache in less than two seconds, anyway?

Taryn blinked back tears. It was stupid. It was wrong. It was impossible. But the only lover she wanted to be with when she finally heard one of her songs on the radio was Brian.

* * *

Whoever said "If you love someone, set them free; if they come back, it's meant to be" was clearly full of crap. That, or a sadist.

The idea of walking out of Brian's hotel room, knowing even if they were meant to be together, the odds were completely against them, had Taryn's belly hurting so badly it was a wonder she could breathe.

Maybe the whole problem with that analogy was the word love. In order for it to apply to them, she would have to love Brian. And clearly she...

Oh, hell, who was she kidding? She did.

She loved him, wanted him. Couldn't stand the thought of leaving him. But she had to. The flight back to Michigan left at ten, and she and Sarah had to be at the airport by eight for check-in. Taryn wanted to find Dawn and say good-bye and get the woman's phone number before leaving. She still had to pack.

She glanced at the clock, the same way she'd done every few seconds since waking up in Brian's arms twenty minutes ago. Almost seven already. She had to leave. Sarah hadn't expected her back last night, but if Taryn didn't show up in their room soon, her friend would panic. If Sarah did that, she would call Brian's room and wake him up.

He couldn't wake up. Leaving was hard enough without having to look him in the face and say good-bye, knowing it was probably forever.

Being careful not to jar him, Taryn brushed a last kiss over his mouth and slid from his arms. She hurried to dress, and then with a last watery-eyed look at the man who had truly turned out to be a nice guy, slipped from the room. She would leave a note for him at the front desk, so he didn't attempt to look for her when he woke up, along with the song he'd been the inspiration behind.

Inspiration.

He'd given her so much in so many different ways. Even if they never spoke again, she'd always have that to be thankful for.

Chapter Twenty-two

"I still think branching out would do wonders for the company."

Taryn didn't bother to swivel in her office chair to look at Sarah. For the three weeks since they'd returned from Sugar Foot, her friend had been trying to convince her opening a Tennessee-based branch of Lasting Impressions was a sound business venture. It might be a sound business venture, but that wasn't the reason Sarah kept bringing it up. No, that would be Brian.

Ick. Just the thought of his name made Taryn's belly go into automatic ache mode. "Drop it already, Sarah. There's no way I'm moving to a state I know nothing about and starting a new company because I had great sex with a guy and now that guy refuses to get out of my head."

"The ballsy Taryn of old would do it."

Yeah, well, the ballsy Taryn of old would have had at least one more lover since returning home from Sugar Foot too, but the new Taryn hadn't. The new Taryn didn't want one more lover. She just wanted her old lover back. "I'm not that Taryn anymore."

"I know," Sarah said smugly. "I've been wondering when you were going to admit it. I've also been wondering when you're going to admit how you feel about Brian."

"I..." Taryn closed her mouth around the denial she'd been about to voice. What was the point of continuing to lie to her best friend? She swiveled in her chair and made a face at Sarah before giving in. "Oh, fine. I fell for him, hook, line, and sinker. I miss him like hell. Are you happy now?"

Sarah frowned. "Not really. I hate seeing you depressed." She brightened then. "You know Laurel was saying she has friends down in Tennessee, think the Bible Belt, who want to open a store similar to the Wiccan Emporium. If there's a place someone would need great promotional help to get a Wicca-themed business off its feet, it would be there."

"And, wow," Taryn said drily "how convenient that Tennessee is where Brian lives."

"That is pretty ironic, isn't it? Some might even say fated."

Taryn never rolled her eyes—that was Sarah's thing—but this time she couldn't stop herself. "Oh, jeez, you've been spending way too much time with Laurel."

"Well, no offense, hon, but you haven't exactly been a ton of fun to hang out with lately." Sarah picked up the phone on her desk and held the receiver out toward Taryn. "Call him, Tare. So you live a long ways apart, you can still talk."

Right, like conversation would ever be enough. "I don't know his number."

"Yeah, and I'm sure it's not somewhere on the Internet. These days everyone's number and most of their vital stats are listed. Google him."

"I don't know."

Sarah set the phone back on the cradle and stood. "I do." She crossed to Taryn's desk and leaned against it with a hand to her hip. "You've got it bad, girl. So bad that you've whined at least five times this week that Chocolate Cashew Heaven no longer tastes as good as it used to. That is a major thing in your book. And, honestly, if it were me in your situation, I would have called him long ago and probably be shacked up by now."

What, was she trying to make her laugh? Whether that had been the intention or not, Taryn couldn't stop her snort of laughter. "Right. You. Ms. I'm-on-lucky-guy-number-eight-and-it's-only-March. Fat chance."

"Actually, nine." Sarah's cherry red lips curved into a pleased smile. "Had a blind date go right last night." She sobered. "And I was speaking metaphorically, like 'if I were you, I would do this.' I'm not the type who can settle down. I don't have those genes."

"Why not? You've said that before, and I didn't get the reason then either."

Sarah's lips formed an irritable pout. With a shrug, she moved back to her desk and sat. "I just don't. There doesn't need to be a reason, and you're trying to change the subject. You need to call him and say the big *L* word, Tare. If you don't"—the slightly naughty smile she always got before she said something Taryn would probably be afraid to hear surfaced—"well, I'll have to take matters into my own hands."

Yep, that was the last thing Taryn wanted to hear.

"Please don't. I'll call him. I will. Just…maybe not till next week."

Or next year.

Or, oooh, not to sound like Laurel, but her next lifetime sounded even better. Well, to her frame of mind it did. The rest of her wanted to call right this second and demand to know why Brian hadn't contacted her long ago.

The big *L* word. She had it bad.

* * *

Taryn surfaced from a dream where a giant Speedy Gonzales had her trapped against a wall and was nibbling on her ear, to the shrill ringing of her telephone.

Groaning over the dream and the obvious correlation of the cartoon mouse to Brian, she glanced at the alarm clock. It was after one in the morning. Who would call this late unless it was an emergency?

Anxiety had her picking the phone up and shouting a hello into the receiver.

"Are you in bed?"

Anxiety turned to anger as the too-familiar male voice caught up with her. Brian had some balls to be calling her after he'd taken another lover less than a month after leaving Sugar Foot. Ache stabbed at

Taryn's belly over the reminder of finally getting up the nerve to call his house only to have a woman answer. A woman who was breathing hard and had assured her Brian was too busy to come to the phone just then, but she could take a message if Taryn wanted.

Like she wanted to leave a message for that prick. "Brian," she said.

"Are you in bed?" he repeated.

"What do you think? It's after one in the morning, and I have to be up for work by six. Why are you calling?" Damn it, she shouldn't have asked that question. It made it sound like she cared. And she didn't care about his sorry ass, not one iota.

"Are you naked?"

Yep, a sorry ass he was, because now he wasn't just messing with her head, but all of her. The thought of being naked while he whispered hot words in her ear through the phone line had her pussy tingling, and her entire body on fire.

Well, fine, she would respond, but he wouldn't like the answer. "Yeah, I am." She purposefully made her voice low, throaty. "I'm lying her naked, basking in postorgasm glow with my guy of the night. Ohhh...Matt," she improvised, pulling the phone away. "You're so good at that!" She waited a beat, then brought the phone back to her mouth. "He's all revved up again, so I got to go. See you—"

Brian laughed. "You don't sound like that when you're aroused, Taryn. Stop lying, and turn on your radio, channel 102.8."

Right, like he was an expert on how she sounded when she was aroused. He might know a little bit, but she still knew better.

Taryn reached to her alarm clock and turned the radio on, but only because appeasing him seemed the best way to get rid of him. If she hung up the phone, he was liable to call right back, and then she'd never get any sleep tonight. As it was, if she managed to fall asleep, it would probably be to dream of a big-eared mouse licking her navel.

"Fine. I'm turning on my radio." She adjusted the dial until it landed on the channel he'd indicated. The trailing lyrics of a popular rock song filled the dark bedroom. "Are you happy now?"

"Just listen."

She listened, to a commercial for a used car lot. "Don't you have something, make that someone, better to…" She paused as the disc jockey's voice replaced the car ad, saying her name.

What the hell? Why was the guy saying her name?

Taryn turned up the volume. She bit her lip as the man announced the next song was going out to her from Brian. The first lyrics of the song had her eyes welling. Tears drenched her cheeks by the final refrain. It wasn't just a cheesy song he'd dedicated to her. It was *her* song. The one she'd given his mother that night backstage at the concert.

"Taryn?" Brian's voice came over the phone line.

She tried to speak through the emotions clogging her throat, but couldn't get a word out.

"Taryn? Are you there? Are you okay?"

No, she wasn't okay. How had he managed to get her song on the radio, and how was it possible it sounded so completely like his mother singing it? Or maybe why was the better word. Why would he go to all that effort when he was sleeping with another woman?

"Taryn, I miss you."

Her heart squeezed tight with the sincerity that seemed to fill his words. She pushed the sensation aside, forced words out. "What are you doing, Brian? How are you doing it? That sounds like...like your mother."

"Do you miss me?"

Too freaking much.

Taryn swallowed back her emotions, the truth of how much she'd missed him the last month. However Brian had managed to get her song on the radio, it was nice of him to do so, but it didn't change the facts. "You don't miss me. If you did, you never would have slept with someone else."

"I don't know what you're talking about, sweetheart. I never slept with anyone else. I don't want to. Can I talk you into coming to see me sometime?"

Sweetheart? And why did he sound so serious, like the idea of sleeping with someone else wasn't even a little bit appealing? "No. It isn't possible."

"That's too bad. I wanted to talk about some things. About us."

Them? He thought there was a "them"? What about that woman who'd answered his phone breathing hard? If she wasn't his lover, then what?

Taryn focused on the song playing on the radio. Her heart was invested in it too, but not so much as it would be if she responded to his words about them. "How did you do this, Brian? How did you find someone who sounds so much like your mother to sing a song you'd never even heard before?"

"I didn't find someone that sounds like my mother. That really is her. She must have listened to that demo tape you gave her the night of the concert and liked what she heard. I found an uncut version of it in a box of things I'd put off going through. Yours wasn't the only one in there, but it was the only one that mattered. I wish I could make your dream complete, Taryn. You told me you weren't alone when you heard your song, remember? Someone else was in your bed."

Yeah, stupidly, she'd put him there. "Brian, I—"

The ringing of her apartment doorbell cut her off.

What was up with this night? First, a middle of the night phone call, and now a middle of the night visitor? Maybe it was Sarah. Maybe lucky guy number ten had turned her down. Right. "Hang on."

Taryn climbed out of bed. She pulled her robe off the hanger on the back of the bedroom door and quickly slipped it on. She flicked on the bedroom lights, then the living room ones, and peered through the peephole of the front door.

Brian stood there, looking back at her, with a cell phone pressed to his ear.

Her heart slammed against her ribs. She thrust the phone back to her ear, gasped, "Brian?"

He smiled. "Sorry it's so late, but I had some business to finish up before I could leave this morning."

"You're here," she mumbled, unable to form any further words.

His smile turned to a sexy half grin. "I am."

"Why?"

He laughed. "Open the door, Taryn. I want to tell you in person."

She shouldn't. It was much safer with him on the outside. Her fingers didn't obey her mind, but quickly unlocked the door and pulled it open. "Why?" she asked again, when he was standing directly in front of her, looking better than any man had a right to look, especially this late at night.

Brian pulled the phone from his ear. His grin melted. "Because I love you."

Well, if that was all...

Taryn's hand shook, and she realized she still held the phone to her ear. She pulled it away and hit the Off button. Took several calming breaths.

Had he honestly just said that he loved her?

"What about the other woman? When I called your house, a woman answered the phone. She was breathing hard."

"Can I come in?"

She thought to say no again, but then nodded. He moved into the apartment, closed the door, and leaned back against it. All those times he'd struck that pose at the conference he looked so sure of himself, confident and casual. Now he looked uncertain and not casual in the least.

"I did a lot of thinking about what you said, about how keeping everyone at a distance wasn't really living. You were right. What's the point if you don't take chances? I called my dad and Pam, my stepmom, a couple weeks ago. They were so relieved to hear from me, they flew out to visit the next day. I'm guessing Pam was the woman who answered the phone." His smile returned, and he feigned a shudder. "As for the heavy breathing, I don't even want to think what might have caused that."

Taryn tried to laugh, but couldn't get the sound out, and knew even if she did, it wouldn't sound authentic. Her emotions were running too rampant. "So there was never another woman?"

"No, Taryn. There's only you."

Tears pushed to the backs of her eyes. This time she did laugh, at her own idiotic behavior. She never used to be a crier, but lately all it took was thoughts of Brian, or apparently, words from Brian, and she felt ready to break down.

He reached a tentative hand toward her. When she didn't back away, he stroked her cheek with the back of his hand. "I never told you about Pam. She's involved in the music industry too. I guess as much as Dad didn't feel he got the attention from Mom he needed, he couldn't quite leave the business behind. Pam helped me get that old song of yours, and a few others Mom never released, into the hands of someone who might be able to do something about it. That version you heard tonight hasn't been picked up yet, but I know it will be. Just like I know that song you left me on the CD will be."

The song he'd been the inspiration behind. Taryn had left the finalized version along with her good-bye note to Brian at the front desk of the Seaside. And he'd believed in her enough to take it and do something with it.

She blinked back tears, smiled. "I really need to stop calling you names."

He chuckled. "Have you been doing that again?"

"When I called your house and Pam answered and it sounded like she'd just crawled out of your bed, I wanted to hate you. I thought I did."

"But you don't?"

"No. I don't." His eyes lit with happiness. She curbed the impulse to throw herself into his arms. There were still things to be said.

"Have I mentioned Sarah's idea about expanding the company? She thinks I should start a Tennessee branch of Lasting Impressions." As much as he seemed happy to see her, Taryn's nerves flared in wait of his response to the idea they could be neighbors, or possibly housemates.

Brian's hand fell from her face, and he pulled her against him, to that spot against his chest she'd missed like crazy. He smiled down at her. "I was wrong about Sarah. She sounds like a very smart woman. You will need a lot of help running the business, though, since you'll be spending most of your time concentrating on your songwriting. And then there's the little matter of keeping your lover, who by the way will be working a lot less hours from now on, happy.

"I have this thing about taking it slow, spending lots of long hours talking, touching, making love. We can go fast sometimes too, of course. I wouldn't want your inner control freak getting ticked off at me. Might have to paddle her ass to put her back in her place."

Laughing, Taryn rose on her tiptoes and brushed a kiss across his mouth. "I like it when your inner control freak takes over."

He rubbed his lips back over hers, slowly. "Yeah?"

"Oh, yeah," she murmured against his mouth, and then dived in headlong, wrapping her arms around his neck and meeting his tongue halfway. Her phone clunked to the floor; his followed.

She remembered then that he was supposed to be doing the controlling, and let him take over. His mouth slanted over hers, his tongue stroked against hers, licked over her teeth, consumed her senses and made every nerve ending stand at attention.

Moving his hands between them, he untied the sash of her robe. Her nipples hardened as his hands came over her breasts. His palms were like ice, hinting at the outside temperature. The cold drew forth her warmth. Liquid heat rushed between her thighs, flared an inferno in her pussy. She squirmed against him, needing him inside her, wanting him buried deep.

Brian lifted her, and she wrapped his legs around his waist. Panting, she broke from his mouth with the intention of telling him where the bedroom was. Then she realized for all the love and honestly he'd given her, she hadn't done the same. "Wait. I have to say something."

"What?"

Taryn laughed at his pained expression, as if stopping kissing her had dealt him a physical blow. "I love you. And no matter if any of my songs ever make it to the radio for real, I don't care, because I know how much you believe in me. More importantly, I believe in myself. Oh, and the bedroom's down the hall. Second door on the left."

He kissed her again, a tender brush, as he started in that direction. He reached the bedroom and set her back on the bed, came down over her with his arms bracing his weight. "You're going to make it, sweetheart. I promise. Until you do, I'm sure I can think of lots of ways to keep you happy."

Taryn raised an eyebrow. "That doesn't happen to be a challenge, does it?"

"You bet." Brian moved aside her hair and lowered his mouth to her ear, blew on the sensitive flesh, then licked a hot, wet path from her breasts to her navel. She shivered, every cell in her body aroused beyond measure. "A challenge I intend to take great pleasure in seeing through, one lick at a time."

 **THE END**

Jodi Lynn Copeland

Jodi Lynn Copeland learned early on that family and friends and love and laughter are the most important ingredients in happiness. While attending Central Michigan University, she discovered her love for writing and that those same ingredients blend for the perfect romance. Over the years and across the genres, Jodi has found that one thing remains the same...a dash of heat and humor and a heaping spoonful of love make for the best recipe of all.

Jodi's novels have received various awards and commendations, including 4½ Star Top Pick reviews from *RT BOOKclub Magazine*, Selection as *Cosmo Magazine*'s Red Hot Read of the month, Recommended Reads from *The Road To Romance* and *Reviewer's International Organization* (RIO), and nominations for such awards as the National Reader's Choice Award, the EPPIE Award, and the Lauries Bookseller's Best.

When not writing, Jodi can be found enjoying the great outdoors with her two little girls, or working away at the day job where she serves as a marketing specialist for a national engineering firm. Look for Jodi's books at bookstores across the country, as well as online at Amazon.com, BarnesandNoble.com, and various other e-vendors.

CPSIA information can be obtained at www.ICGtesting.com
Printed in the USA
LVOW131627270812

296157LV00003B/129/P

9 781611 183948